Christmas at Saltwater Cove

Press

Pittsburgh

Christmas at Saltwater Cove

ANJ Press, First edition. October 2020.
Written by Amelia Addler.

Cover design by Charmaine Ross at CharmaineRoss.com
Maps by Nate Taylor at IllustratorNate.com

for Argos

Introduction to *Christmas at Saltwater Cove*

The ghosts of relationships past are threatening her happily ever after...

Pediatric surgeon Sandy Randall has given up on love. At 53, with a divorce and a string of bad dates behind her, she just doesn't see the point of it. Besides, her career keeps her way too busy to worry about romance. But when a trip to San Juan Island brings her face-to-face with her high school sweetheart, she can't help but wonder how the icy walls she's built around her heart can possibly survive him again.

Jack Pappas is thrilled when a holiday catering gig puts him back in contact with Sandy. In his mind, she was the one that got away – and she's more beautiful and delightful than ever. All he'll have to do now is convince her to give him (and love) a second chance...

Somewhere between the caroling and mistletoe (and the unwanted medical mystery that hits San Juan Island), can Jack and Sandy figure out how to take one last shot at love? It might take a Christmas miracle...

This story works as a stand alone that fits into the Westcott Bay series right after book one (*Saltwater Cove*), however whether you've read all of the Westcott Bay books or none at all, this story is the perfect holiday pick-me-up!

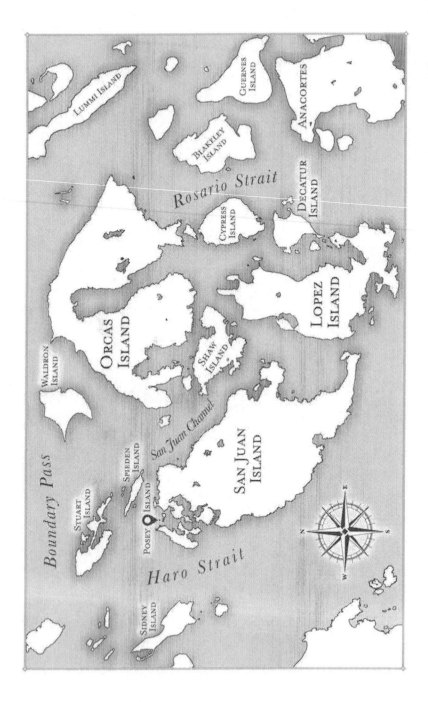

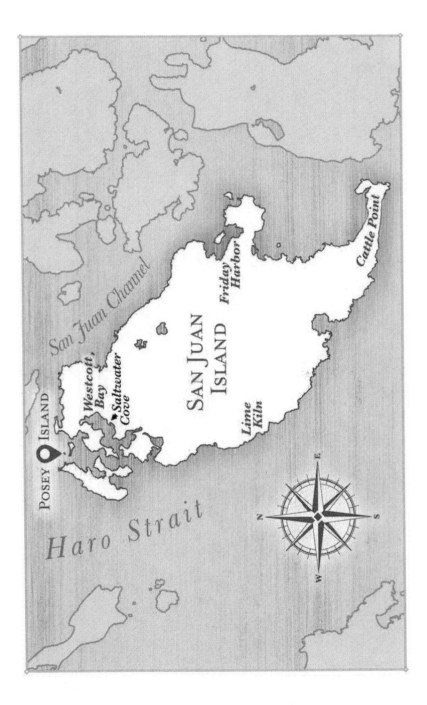

Chapter 1

"We're next for takeoff. Get ready to have some fun!"

Sandy smiled, but couldn't manage to do much else. The small Cessna plane sat at the end of the runway, the long strip of cement beckoning them to move forward. Meanwhile, her body was completely stiff – something she hadn't expected. Perhaps it was too bold an idea for her to sit in the front with the pilot.

He'd offered, though, and this wasn't her first rodeo. She'd seen this view of the cockpit before – the dials and knobs of the control panel, the oversized headsets, and the propeller's dizzying spin breaking up her view. She'd heard the impossibly loud engine roaring to life before, and remembered how the vibrations rattled through her entire body.

But during her many previous flights, her brother Mike was the pilot. Not a stranger. She didn't even know this guy. What was his name? Bill?

Brett?

No, definitely Bill.

He was too young to be a pilot – he looked like he'd just graduated college.

"You know..." she said into her headset, "if the weather doesn't look good, we can just go back and I'll rent a car..."

He laughed. "Don't worry, it's a perfect day. And we'll be in the air in no time."

Bill started talking through a checklist and Sandy had no choice but to leave him alone.

She vaguely remembered that Mike had used a checklist like that when he flew. Yet she hadn't been scared like this – and Sandy wasn't used to feeling scared. She wasn't a jittery person by any means – yet here she was, wondering if the flimsy latch on her door would pop open and send her tumbling out.

The plane started rumbling down the runway. Sandy couldn't believe what she'd gotten herself into. Why hadn't she just rented a car like she initially planned?

Oh right – because her sister Margie insisted that she couldn't be late and miss Santa's arrival. She said it was the "Perfect kick-off to a month of Christmas fun!"

What did Sandy care about Santa? She had no interest in the man. What use could a fifty-three year old woman with no children have for a sweaty man in a red suit?

None!

She should've rented a car at the airport, driven to the ferry terminal, and taken the ferry to San Juan Island like a normal person.

"Oh dear..." she whispered as the plane lifted off of the runway.

It wasn't the smooth, gradual ascent of a commercial airliner. No – one moment it was bumping along the runway like an old, oddly shaped car, and the next moment it popped up into the air, like it was a toy and not a real plane.

But that was it – they were flying! She let out a sigh; everything seemed fine. She'd allowed herself to get too worked up.

The world shrank beneath them and Sandy decided that if she was going to die in this plane, she might as well enjoy the view. She delicately leaned to her right to look out of the window. Her hope was to see Seattle as they flew by, but it seemed they were already plunging deep into the clouds.

"That wasn't so bad, was it?" asked Bill.

Sandy laughed. "That's one way to think of it. We got an amazing view for a minute."

"Just wait until we get to the islands!" he said. "It should clear up a bit and you'll get the view of a lifetime."

Sandy forced herself to release her grip on the armrest. "Great."

"Is this your first time flying in a small aircraft?"

"No. I used to fly with my brother all the time."

Bill looked over to her. "Oh – but not any more?"

"No, he had to move for his job." Sandy forced herself not to smile. That was one way to put it. Mike went back undercover with the FBI. Sometimes she had the urge to tell people that, just to see their reaction. But she knew she couldn't.

"I see. And you're going to San Juan for business, or pleasure?"

"I'm visiting my sister. My brother actually sold her his house on San Juan Island."

"No way! Lucky lady."

Sandy nodded. Surely Margie thought of it that way – she was a stunningly positive person. But it hadn't been so lucky when Margie's husband left her out of the blue. And after twenty-two years of raising their children and keeping their home in order, she had nothing to show for it.

But everything changed after Mike gave her that house.

"Yeah, it's wonderful – right on the water. She turned an old barn into a wedding venue. Or an events space, I guess. That's all the rage now."

"Oh yeah! My daughter got married in a barn last summer. No air conditioning, but it was nice."

Daughter? He looked so young – maybe it was the sunglasses? Or maybe Sandy was losing her touch in guessing ages. Or maybe...

Sandy stole a glance at him again. He had some gray hair and even a few wrinkles. Somehow she'd missed that when she first met him – probably because her mind was preoccupied.

The flight was short at only thirty-five minutes. She couldn't complain about that. If she'd driven up and taken the ferry over, it would've taken her at least three hours – maybe five hours with traffic. She was already quite bored of traveling after her flight from Boston.

And as promised, when they got closer to the San Juan Islands, they had a magnificent view.

"Do you see that?" Bill pointed. "Right there is Orcas Island. That peak is Mount Constitution – twenty-four hundred feet tall! And down below us we've got Lopez island."

"It's beautiful."

She meant it. The islands always took her breath away – no matter how many times she'd seen them and no matter the vantage point.

Squinting, she could make out a few boats scurrying on the water. The islands themselves were blots of green, covered in thick swathes of trees. Occasionally where the trees cleared, she could make out patches of fields or little farms. It looked so underdeveloped and peaceful, much calmer and less crowded than the city she'd just left behind.

She didn't have long to enjoy the view though; within a few minutes they approached the runway of the airport.

Sandy now regretted that she'd spent so much of the trip feeling afraid. She didn't usually let herself get worked up like that – though in her defense, this was a new situation.

In her work as a surgeon, she could watch others panic and all the while keep her cool – but only because she'd been through it a hundred times before.

She felt the plane drop, but didn't see the runway until it was right in front of them. Just like with takeoff, the plane plopped down rather unceremoniously. Within moments, they'd slowed and found a place to park.

"Welcome to San Juan Island, our high temperature today is fifty degrees," Bill said as he shut off the plane.

"Only three weeks until Christmas and it's *still* that warm?" Sandy peeked out of the window. There was no snow and the island looked as green and lovely as she remembered.

"It never gets too cold here. Best weather in the world," he added with a smile. "Thank you for flying with us today, I hope to see you again."

"It was *really* nice, thank you."

"Great. Here – I'll help you out." He jumped out of his seat and ran around the plane to open her door and fetch her bags.

"I can walk you into the airport. Do you have anyone here to pick you up?"

"I do," Sandy said. "My sister Margie."

As soon as they walked in the doors, there was a scream from the other side of the airport.

"*Over here!*"

There stood Margie and her daughter Jade, waving a large sign.

"Thanks Bill. I think I have the loudest welcome party in the entire airport."

"I think you have the *only* welcome party in the airport. Have fun – and have a Merry Christmas!"

"You too!"

Margie continued calling and gleefully waving a sign that read, "All I want for Christmas is my sister Sandy to visit!"

She laughed to herself. For a moment when she first saw the sign, she thought it might be a joke – something like "Welcome home from prison!"

But Margie didn't do things like that; it was far more likely that her kids would pull that sort of prank. It was a good idea, though; Sandy made a mental note to remember to make a sign like that for Margie the next time she came to Boston.

"You made it!" Margie said once she got closer.

"I did. It's so good to see you!" She hugged Margie, then Jade.

Jade was beaming. "We're so excited to have you, Aunt Sandy!"

"Now I'm sure that you're probably tired from your travels," Margie said as she wrestled Sandy's suitcase into her own grip. "But we have about an hour before Santa arrives in Friday Harbor. So if you're up for it, we can run home, change and do whatever you need to do, and then we'll head out."

"That sounds perfect."

"Come on Mom," said Jade. "Aunt Sandy's a surgeon. She doesn't get tired. You work, like, forty-eight hour shifts, right?"

Sandy laughed. "Sometimes. But I definitely feel it more now that I'm older."

Margie waved a hand. "Nonsense! You don't look a day over thirty-five."

"Right back at you."

They hopped into Margie's car, chatting the whole time. It'd been a while since Sandy visited the island, and nothing looked quite familiar. As they gabbed, she took in the rolling farms and glimpses of the shore between the lush trees.

It wasn't until they were riding along the coast that Sandy really recognized something. The shoreline was unchanged – her eyes traced the rocky, jagged edges of the island; the raw power of the water crashing in, again and again.

Goosebumps rippled over her arms; she remembered standing on those rocks years ago, the sea mist spraying her face. It was her first time on the island – she'd visited right when her brother bought his house. Sandy was at a crossroads then, thinking of leaving her surgery residency and starting over.

Thankfully, she didn't do that. It was the right choice.

They pulled up to the house and before Sandy could even get out of the car, Margie made off with her bag. Once inside, Sandy realized that the house also looked nothing like she remembered. The interior was completely redone and rather tastefully decorated.

Mike had never decorated the house when he lived there – he sort of neglected it, really. It was clearly in much better hands with Margie.

Their first stop was the kitchen, where Margie had prepared a number of Sandy's favorite things – Thai chicken wings on a stick, taco burger sliders, and stuffed figs with honey.

"Margie, you shouldn't have done all of this!" Sandy shook her head. "I thought you said that we were going to eat in town?"

"Well, these were just a couple of *little* things I wanted you to have," Margie explained. "I didn't want you to starve to death!"

Sandy smiled. As though *anyone* could starve around Margie – she was an accomplished chef, baker and an over-whelmingly considerate hostess.

Even when Sandy was invited to speak at a conference at a fancy five-star hotel, their service didn't hold a candle to her own sister. No one could make her feel more at home or more loved. With Margie, no detail went undone – from her favorite foods waiting for her when she walked in the door, to the water bottle and bowl of her favorite candy (peanut butter M&Ms) at her bedside table.

Margie was something else.

Sandy was used to eating while standing, so she stacked a plate with goodies and followed Margie for a quick tour.

They started with the house and then moved outside. As they approached the barn, Sandy saw a hand-painted wooden sign that read, "The Barn at Saltwater Cove."

She smiled. It was perfect. She could see why people wanted to get married here. Once inside, she was awed that this once run-down barn now looked like something out of a maga-zine.

"Margie this is *really* impressive."

She beamed. "You think so? Well, thank you. I've had a lot of help."

"I'm honestly stunned. When you said you were having weddings here I thought – well, I don't know what I thought. I guess it's been a long time since I've been to a wedding, but I thought it would look like a fire hall or something. But this – this is gorgeous!"

"Oh stop, you're going to make me blush!"

"How has business been?"

Margie sighed. "It's been a little slow to start, but not bad. We hosted an office Christmas party last weekend."

"Oh, and how did that go?"

"I thought it went well," she said. "But apparently one of the organizers, Edgar Tucker, is telling people that the barn was dirty, and that he got sick from the food. Or no – he blamed the water."

"What! That's ridiculous."

"It's making me a little nervous. The barn wasn't dirty, not in the least! I cleaned everything myself. I'm afraid that if we get a bad reputation...well, I can't worry about that. I hope that with more time, things will get better."

"I'm sure they will."

"And in order to get Saltwater Cove's name out there, I'm hosting a Christmas cookie contest next weekend."

Sandy laughed. "Of course you are. Be honest – you just wanted an excuse to have your own Christmas party."

"Nonsense," Margie said with a smile. "Don't you like Christmas cookies?"

"As long as I don't have to make them, yes."

"Well don't worry," she said. "I'd never force your to bake. I was actually hoping that you'd agree to be one of the judges."

"Oh, *now* you're talking! I'm in." Sandy stopped to look at her watch. "Shouldn't we get going?"

Margie gasped. "Oh my! Yes! Let me find Jade and we'll go."

They got back to the car and drove to Friday Harbor. It looked like the whole island was getting into the holiday spirit – the sidewalks were brimming with happy little families, sipping on hot cocoa and snacking on freshly fried churros.

As they made their way to the docks, Margie apologized that it was "so cold." That made Sandy laugh out loud – when she'd left Boston, it was blanketed with over four inches of snow. San Juan Island felt positively balmy.

After getting hot cider and cookies, they got to the docks to watch the parade of ships escorting Santa's boat into the harbor.

Sandy squinted. "Which one is he on?"

"The one that says 'Santa is coming' with those big banners," Jade said with a laugh.

Sandy finally spotted the bushy bearded man standing at the helm of the ship, waving. It was close enough to hear now – the speakers on the ship blasting "Jingle Bells," much to the delight of the children screaming and waving from the dock.

Sandy smiled to herself – it was certainly the most unique way she'd ever seen Santa make an entrance.

As soon as the ship docked, Santa walked down, patting his belly and shouting, "Merry Christmas!"

Within moments, he was surrounded by children who took him by the hands and led him up the dock.

"Where are they going?" asked Sandy.

"Ah," said Jade. "The historical society has a chair set up for Santa so the kids can get their pictures taken and tell him what they want for Christmas."

"All right Margie." Sandy sighed. "You were right."

"About what?"

"It was definitely worth making it here early so I could see that. It was adorable."

Margie smiled. "I'm glad to hear you say that."

"Where to now?" asked Sandy. "Is there caroling? Or ornament decorating? Or..."

Sandy paused. At the end of the dock, just behind the crowd of children, a man stood waving. Was he looking at them?

"Do you know that guy? He looks oddly familiar but I can't place him..."

"Isn't that..." said Jade slowly.

Margie cut her off. "Oh my gosh, would you look at that! If I didn't know any better, I'd say that looks like Jack Pappas!"

Sandy turned to her. "What? That doesn't make any sense."

"Wait," said Jade. "Is he the guy we met last week, Mom? At that restaurant in Seattle and you said – "

Sandy cleared her throat. "Let me guess, your mom remembered him from high school?"

"Yeah!" replied Jade.

"Did she also tell you that he was my high school boyfriend?"

"Hello Jack!" Margie called out, waving and walking toward him.

Sandy wanted to say something to her, but she was already halfway down the dock.

She let out a sigh.

No, her sister hadn't met her at the airport with a prank sign. She went and did something *much* more embarrassing – Margie went and found her high school boyfriend and somehow dragged him all the way to San Juan Island.

Chapter 2

Santa Claus, engulfed in a swarm of kids, steadily moved up the dock and onto the street. Jack stood watching and thinking of his own daughter; where had the time gone? He could close his eyes and see her in his mind's eye, age six, excited about Santa like it was yesterday.

And now she was married and having her own kid!

He let out a sigh and gazed out onto the water. Such was life, always moving too fast for his tastes. Perhaps this trip was a mistake – instead of being alone at home on Christmas like he'd initially planned, he'd be alone and in a strange place. The thought of it hung on him like a weight.

But before he got too lost in thought, something caught his eye – at the end of the dock, near Santa's ship, was Margie and her daughter Jade. And as promised, Sandy was with them too.

The weight pressing on his chest lifted and a smile spread across his face.

When Jack had run into Margie last week in Seattle, he couldn't believe his luck. He hadn't seen her in over twenty years and she just appeared, as if by magic.

"Jack! My daughter Jade showed me an article in the paper and I recognized you instantly! I can't believe that this wonderful restaurant is *yours*! And we just had to come and see for ourselves."

He smiled. "Yes, Jade's right. But after this week, it's no longer going to be my restaurant."

"It's nice to meet you," said Jade. She had the same delicate features of her mother, but her voice was much softer.

"Right!" Margie continued. "You've sold it? Successful, and you're famous too."

"I wouldn't go that far," he said with a laugh. "But the paper did a very nice write up about the restaurant. It's really taken on a life of its own."

"Why did you decide to sell it? Do you have something else in the works?" asked Margie.

"Not exactly. My daughter, Helen, moved out to Massachusetts. She's married now, and expecting her first child this spring. I wanted to be closer to her, so – I'm moving!"

"Oh how lovely! And how's Susan?"

"You have a good memory," Jack replied. "Susan's good. And actually – well, we're not together anymore. We split up about two years ago."

"I'm sorry to hear that."

It was always awkward telling people about the divorce, but there was no nastiness between them. Nearly thirty years of marriage was still a success in his book. They'd just grown apart. "It's quite all right."

Margie smiled. "And that's exciting – moving across the country! Are you planning on spending Christmas with Helen?"

He shook his head. "Not this year. She's spending the holiday with her husband and in-laws – down in Florida. I'm actually on my own this Christmas."

"Well we can't allow that," Margie said, setting down her fork. "Listen, I just moved to San Juan Island. I have a little barn where I'm hosting a Christmas cookie contest in two weeks, and I just *cannot* find a caterer. And seeing that you're not busy, what would you think of coming to the island for a little work vacation?"

Jack chuckled. "Well that's a very enticing offer, but – "

Margie continued. "Plus, the island has all kinds of lovely Christmas activities – I'm sure there are plenty of places to stay, too. Actually, I know a place. I could get you a deal. And, who knows, you could reconnect with some old friends?"

He didn't know what she meant by old friends, but he wasn't interested in being the lonely guy on an island of happy people. "Oh – that's very nice of you. I'll think about it."

Margie's stare on him was unbroken. "Did I mention that Sandy is coming to visit for the whole month of December?"

Oh.

Now she had his attention. He hadn't spoken to Sandy since he went to college – and she dumped him.

"Really? The whole month?"

Jade giggled. "It's a funny story. She got called into an emergency surgery, and then – "

"Did something happen to her?" asked Jack.

"No, no – nothing bad happened," Margie waved a hand. "It wasn't *her* surgery. She's a surgeon. A pediatric surgeon."

"Oh! I didn't know that." Jack was never able to find out much about Sandy after they'd broken up. He'd get the occasional news from his mom – that she was going to medical school, that she'd gotten married – but it seemed that Sandy never wanted to reconnect or catch up with him.

"You know," Margie went on, "she's *also* divorced! Well – not as recently. It's been about...oh, I guess seventeen years."

"Ah." Jack rubbed the back of his neck. He knew what Margie was doing. She was never a subtle person, and it seemed that it wasn't a skill she'd managed to refine in the past few decades. Not that he wasn't flattered, but...

He cleared his throat. "Well, I'm sure that – "

"Oh come on Jack, just think about it." Margie said with a smile. "The island could be a great getaway for you. And I *really* need someone to make appetizers for my party. It wouldn't be anything too cumbersome. I'll be the talk of the island, having a famous chef from Seattle catering my party. You'd be doing me a huge favor!"

"Well..." Jack knew that if he stayed at their table any longer, there was no telling what he might agree to. "I don't want to take up any more of your time here – but let me get your phone number and maybe we can talk about it later?"

Margie clapped her hands together. "Deal."

Initially, he had no intention of going to San Juan Island for Christmas and fully planned on making up an excuse as to why he couldn't come.

But after he thought about it, he realized that he had nothing to lose. He had nowhere to go, and no one to see. It was his first Christmas alone and he was really dreading it.

At least Margie was a friendly face. And it would be nice to see Sandy – just to talk to her again and catch up. Truth be told, though, it made him feel nervous.

It was odd. It even made him a little...giddy? Over the years, he often wondered what happened to her. When she'd broken up with him, it destroyed him. He spent the first year of college trying to win her back, but she had none of it. Once Sandy made up her mind about something, it was final.

And now, over thirty years later, there she was, standing at the end of the dock. He couldn't help himself – he stood there, waving like an idiot.

Margie was the first to meet him. "I'm so glad you made it! I'm hoping that you found a nice place to stay?"

Jack nodded, tearing his eyes away from Sandy. "I did actually, thank you. I even have a great kitchen for cooking."

"Great!" Margie turned around. "Oh, there you are! You two are so slow today."

"Hi Jade, it's nice to see you again," said Jack.

"It's nice to see you too."

He turned to Sandy, who was studying him with a bemused smile.

He couldn't believe it. She looked the same. A bit older, sure, but still *her*. Even the flat look that she was giving him made him feel like he'd time traveled – like he'd just seen her yesterday.

"How are you, Sandy?"

"I'm very well. How are you?"

He took in a deep breath. The melancholy that was rapidly engulfing him only moments before was now being washed away. Maybe it was all the sugar? "Good. No – great! I've had three cups of hot cocoa and half a dozen cookies."

Margie laughed. "You know that we have regular food on the island, right?"

He nodded. "Yes, I do. I was just walking around, enjoying the lights and all of the festivities. I guess I just got a little carried away."

"Well," Margie clasped her hands together. "How about you two go ahead and get a table for dinner? After Santa is done hearing what the kids want for Christmas, he comes and dines with everyone. Jade and I will join you in just a bit – we have to...find my fiancé Hank."

"Oh?" said Sandy.

Margie waved a hand, already walking away. "Yes, I'm sure he's around here somewhere. We'll be back really soon! Go get some real food!"

Jack waited until Margie was out of earshot to say, "Well, I'm sorry about all of this, but she's *your* sister."

Sandy burst into laughter.

Jack smiled to himself – her laugh was exactly like he remembered. Forceful, loud, and gone in an instant. Like her.

"No, I'm sorry," Sandy said. "I had no idea that she was going to – "

"You don't have to apologize." He shook his head. "Trust me – she really twisted my arm to get me to come to the island. Normally I would try to keep some sort of dignity and not do as I'm told, but she's very convincing."

"She is," Sandy replied.

"Also, I can never miss a chance to make myself sick with enormous cookies," he continued. "I'm perfectly content with getting a table by myself if you'd like to rejoin them."

Sandy studied him for a moment. "No – we should probably get something to eat now. I'm sure you're about to crash from all that sugar."

He laughed. "You're probably right. And we can't miss dinner with Santa – it's a once in a lifetime opportunity."

"It really is," she said with a smile, turning to walk up the street.

As painful and obvious as Margie's matchmaking was, Jack was glad he'd survived it. He was happy just to see Sandy again. Maybe this trip wasn't a mistake after all.

Chapter 3

They got to the restaurant and the hostess offered either a table with a view of the water, or one that would be close to Santa.

"But I have to warn you," she said, "Santa won't be here for at least another hour or two."

"We'll take the table with the view, please," said Sandy. She dropped her voice, adding, "And I'll deal with the wrath of my sister if she complains."

"That only seems fair," Jack replied, waiting so that she could walk ahead of him to the table.

Sandy had to hand it to Margie – she hadn't seen this coming at all. She wasn't even sure how Margie had managed to find Jack – she'd have to ask her about it later.

Not that it *really* mattered – Sandy had no interest in a love affair. She'd tried her hand at love a few times and it never worked out.

To be polite, she'd chat with Jack for a bit; it'd be nice to catch up. Plus, if she did anything less, Margie wouldn't give her a moment's peace for the entirety of her visit. At least with this dinner she could make a quick exit when things started to get boring.

They took their seats and were handed single-paged menus. Sandy frowned. "It looks like they have a special menu just for tonight. Ho–ho–hot cross buns? Candy cane salad? That can't be right."

Jack rubbed his chin. "I think it says that the candy canes come on the side. And look! The pork chop platter comes with a marshmallow snowman."

"Oh good, you'll get to keep your sugar high through dinner. I think I'm going to get the North Pole soup and half reindeer-flavored ham sandwich."

"Excellent choice," he said. "I am going to order the ginger-bread mansion."

Sandy picked up her menu again. "You're kidding! Is that really on there?"

"No, unfortunately not. But I will get the pork chop just so I can see that snowman."

Their waitress checked back in with them and they placed their orders. Sandy also asked for a cup of coffee. She had to decline the additions of a peppermint spoon, a solid chocolate Santa, and marshmallows.

"Well aren't you picky," Jack said after the waitress left.

She laughed. "It's not every day that there are more options than cream and sugar."

"Won't that keep you up all night? Having coffee this late?"

"No, I doubt it'll have any effect at all," Sandy said. "I drink a lot of coffee."

He sat back. "That's right – Margie told me that you're a surgeon? Forgive me that I didn't know, but I never found a way to keep in touch."

"It's okay, I didn't either."

The truth was a bit more complicated than that. She could have stayed in touch with him if she wanted to. But it was too hard. She knew herself, even then – it would have been too easy for him to convince her to give their relationship another try.

And Jack, though he didn't look it now, was always a mischief-maker. Her mom used to call him a "free spirit."

Together they had a lot of fun, but Jack was a little *too* free, and Sandy was too willing to go along with his schemes.

No matter how much she loved him, he was trouble and she knew that he'd hold her back – or rather, they'd hold each other back. She needed to cut all contact if she wanted to move on and do anything with her life.

And when he went away to school, that was exactly what she did.

"What made you want to go into medicine?"

"Oh. It's been a while since anyone asked me that." Sandy let out a sigh and sat back. "Do you remember Betty Cruise?"

He nodded. "I think so. She was your little neighbor?"

"Right. I used to babysit her all the time after you left for college. At the time I was still trying to figure out what to do with my life, and I spent a lot of time hanging around the house or babysitting. One day I was out doing some shopping when I came across a horrible car crash in town."

"I remember hearing about this," he said.

She nodded. "It was Betty and her dad, and their car was hit so hard that it flipped over, stuck on its roof. It morphed into such a horribly twisted pile of metal that I was sure they couldn't have survived. I went home and cried my eyes out."

"I thought that they made it?"

"They did," Sandy said with a smile. "Somehow, they got to the hospital in time and there was a surgery team ready for them. I couldn't believe it when I heard the news; I had to go to the hospital to see for myself. It truly seemed like a miracle to see Betty sitting up in bed when I got there, eating ice cream."

Jack crossed his arms. "Don't make me cry."

"I won't." Sandy held up a hand. "I'm not trying to get mushy on you. But I spent almost two years adrift after graduating high school. I sort of...wandered around from job to job with no idea of what I wanted to do. Until that day. That was the moment I decided that I was going to be a surgeon."

"Wow. That's amazing. And it's so much cooler than what I did."

That made Sandy laugh. "You started a restaurant – that's pretty cool."

He shook his head. "Yes, but it's not where I *really* started. I went to school and graduated with a degree in history. I got married, we found out that we were pregnant with our daughter Helen, and I needed to find a stable job."

Sandy accepted her coffee from the waitress, wrapping her hands around the mug. It was almost too hot to hold, but she didn't want to let go if she could stand it – it made this little table feel even more cozy.

She leaned forward to make sure that she heard every word of the story. "Jack Pappas in a stable job? I don't believe it."

"Well hang onto your hat. The next thing I knew, I got a job at an insurance company."

"No!" Sandy said with a groan. "*You?*"

"It's true," he said. "I was an insurance salesman. For over twenty-five years."

She set down her mug. "I honestly can't believe it. Motorcycle riding, leather jacket wearing Jack Pappas grew up to be an insurance salesman?"

"Hey now, I can still ride a motorcycle."

Sandy laughed. "I'm sure you can. And it's a perfectly respectable job. I just – I don't know, I thought that you would become a professional skydiver or deep-sea welder or something."

"I thought so too. But now that I have you here, I've been meaning to ask you – what kind of life insurance policy do you have? Did you know that – "

Sandy burst out laughing. "Please, make it stop."

"All this time I've led you to believe that Margie convinced me to come here, when really, I've tricked all of *you* to come to my insurance seminar."

"Stop!" She waved a hand through her laughter.

He smiled. "I'm just kidding. But yes – that's what I did. All those years, though, I dreamt of opening my own restaurant. And one day, I looked around. No one was home. I was going to the same job, day in and day out. Our daughter Helen moved away and moved on with her life. I realized that she didn't need me, not like that, anymore. And I just decided to start trying my hand at cooking."

"And what made you make that decision?"

He sat back. "It was...a long time coming. My wife thought that it was a midlife crisis. And at times, it seemed like that. I still went to my day job, but on weekends and evenings, I worked and trained under a famous chef – a guy I knew from college."

"Ah I see. And *then* you started the restaurant."

He nodded. "Yes. And shockingly, though most restaurants fail in their first years, mine was a success. That's where I saw Margie, actually. It was my last week there – I just sold the place. As much as I love it, I don't love being so far away from my daughter."

"Helen?"

"Yes. She's married with a baby on the way. And I don't want to miss out on any time with her, so I'm moving out close to her. She lives in Framingham, it's just outside – "

Sandy smiled. "Of Boston?"

"Yes! You know of it?"

"Yes. I've lived in Boston for years. What about your wife?"

He cleared his throat. "My *ex*-wife. The restaurant was sort of the nail in the coffin. We divorced two years ago."

"I see."

He settled back into his seat. "Do you have any kids?"

There it was. The question that she detested most – but she had her answer ready. "No. But I went on to specialize in pediatric surgery after residency. So sometimes I feel like I have hundreds of kids."

He laughed. "Yes, you've given hundreds of lives."

She always used that line with people – it shut them up pretty quickly.

But Jack wasn't pressing for more information.

After a moment, he added, "I always wanted to have more kids, but we weren't able to."

Did he remember how much she loved children? She finished her last sip of her coffee. "Life never seems to go the way we imagined. But we can't let our expectations hold us back."

"Tell me about it. And we're going to need some eggnog before delving into any more history." He put a hand up to call the waitress over.

She laughed – she wasn't sure that she should discuss more of her history with him, but he seemed more than willing to share his own.

The waitress came over, the bells on her outfit jingling with each step. "How is everything?"

"Everything is wonderful," he said. "Except we're running at a complete deficit of eggnog. And before you ask, here is my ID."

Sandy covered her laughter with her hand before adding, "I'll take an eggnog as well, please."

"Coming right up!" the waitress said, spinning on her heel.

"That should help," he said, leaning in. "When Margie tried to entice me to come to the island, she told me you were divorced. So she's already given away a lot of your history."

"And that enticed you?" Sandy sat back and crossed her arms.

He shrugged. "Of course. I thought it'd be nice to see you. And so far, I'm having a much better time with you than I would have had sitting back in my apartment by myself."

"Well I'm glad I don't disappoint."

"Not at all. Though I am waiting to hear the story of how you ended up on San Juan Island this Christmas."

Sandy narrowed her eyes. "What have you heard?"

"Jade provided some information."

"It's not what you think." Sandy crossed her arms. "I've never done anything like this before."

The waitress stopped by and dropped off two glasses of eggnog. Jack took a sip and immediately said, "When you have a chance, can you please bring two more glasses? This is phenomenal."

She nodded and set off.

"It can't be *that* good," said Sandy.

"Go ahead. Try it."

"I don't usually drink alcohol," she said. "I need to stay sharp."

"Just try it," he said. "I don't think you'll be doing any surgeries tonight."

"True." She took a sip. "Wow. That *is* delicious. It's so creamy and fluffy – what's in there? This is a dumb question, but are there really eggs?"

"I have no idea. I just want to keep them coming."

Sandy laughed and took another taste. "So is this your plan to get me talking? To get me drunk on eggnog?"

"I think you mean drunk on holiday cheer." He paused. "Is it working?"

"Sort of." She set down her glass. That drink was *too* good. "All right, so here's the full story. Last month I was called in for an emergency surgery. It was a school bus accident – we had six kids brought to our emergency room. I had just walked into clinic when I got the call."

He cocked his head to the side. "Clinic?"

She nodded. "Yeah – my post-surgery clinic. So after I do a procedure, I see the kid and the parents for a follow up."

"Oh, of course. Sorry, I'm stupid, move on."

"You're not stupid. Well anyway – I get to the hospital, and they'd already initiated the disaster protocol. Everything was running smoothly, and I was just one part of the machine. I got into the operating room, worked on two of the kids, and thankfully, all of them pulled through."

"That's amazing!"

"Yeah, it was. One of the kids barely had a pulse when they rolled him in, he'd lost so much blood. I was terrified we would lose him."

Jack cleared his throat. "Okay, starting to get me choked up again. I can't imagine what it was like for those kids. Or their parents."

"It's hard. It's always hard. But there's nothing better than a successful surgery." She paused. She didn't want to sound overly grand, so she left it at that. "Anyway, all of the patients I had scheduled in clinic that afternoon had to be rescheduled. The next week, I saw one of the patients – a kid whose appendix I took out. Her mom started screaming at me – how dare I cancel their appointment on short notice, and that she was going to report me to the medical board."

"Sounds reasonable," Jack said with a smile, finishing his first eggnog.

"And I'm not proud of this," Sandy said, taking another sip of her own drink. It was making her feel rather warm. "But after explaining to her that we had an emergency, and apologizing and going on and on...I *might* have yelled at her, just a little bit. I kind of...lost my temper and told her to sit down and be quiet."

He stared at her. "So?"

"What do you mean 'so?' I've never done that in the entire course of my career!"

"What, you can't yell at people every once in a while?"

Sandy laughed. "There's a reputation for some surgeons that they like to yell at everyone. But I've always thought surgery needed nice people, too, and I try my best to be kind."

"And it sounds like you tried to be nice first, but that didn't work."

"Like I said, I'm not proud of it. And then..." she groaned. "I had to have a meeting with the head of surgery and the CEO of the hospital, and it was decided that I was overdue for a vacation..."

He chuckled. "So you're in timeout? Because you yelled at a rude mom?"

"That makes it sound so...silly. But it wasn't silly. What I did was wrong, and I feel awful. I don't know what got into me."

"It sounds like no one got hurt – except maybe that mom's ego. And maybe you needed a vacation after all."

She frowned. It'd been a while since she took a break, but that was no excuse. Maybe she had been too focused on work. They were always talking about burnout, and sure, sometimes she could see needing a break. But she loved her job. She didn't *want* to be someone who had to take a break.

Yet here she was.

"You need to keep up here doc, or I'm going to drink all of these." He pushed the second glass of eggnog toward her. "And I, for one, am glad that you gave her the business like that and ended up here with me."

For the first time since "the incident," she was able to laugh about it. Maybe he was right. No one was hurt, at least. And she'd certainly learned her lesson.

And somehow, it was all a little bit less terrible after sharing it with Jack at this ridiculous restaurant between these ridiculously cozy drinks.

Chapter 4

On Saturday morning, Margie was already working on breakfast when Jade wandered into the kitchen.

"Morning Mom."

"Good morning sweetheart!"

"Where's Aunt Sandy? Is she still sleeping?"

Margie shook her head, pulling a quiche out of the oven. "No, she doesn't sleep in. I think she woke up around five o'clock – she left a note that she didn't want to wake us, so she went out for a walk."

Jade looked around. "And she's still not back?"

"Not yet. But I'm betting that she can't be much longer. At least I hope not – I don't want her to miss breakfast."

"So...are you sure that she's not mad at us?"

Margie stopped what she was doing. "Of course she's not mad! Why would she be?"

"Because," Jade said, "we kind of surprised her with her ex-boyfriend."

"No, it wasn't like that." Margie frowned. "Why, did she say something to you?"

"No, but it didn't seem like she was happy to see him."

"Aha!" Margie said, putting up a finger. "But then she had dinner with him and didn't get home until really late! So she must've had a nice time."

Jade crossed her arms. "I don't know, what if she was just mad at us and that's why she didn't come home until late? And another thing – is that the only reason that you wanted to go to that restaurant with me? After I showed you the article? I just thought that the restaurant looked cool! Aunt Sandy is going to think I was in on this!"

Margie turned around to wash some dishes. "Don't worry honey, you're the innocent party here. I didn't have it all planned out or anything. I mean – I recognized him when you showed me that article. And I thought it would be nice to see him again, and go to the restaurant with you. It was a fun girls day."

"It was..." Jade said slowly. She looked unconvinced.

Margie continued. "But no, I didn't know that he was divorced or anything. Or that he would be spending Christmas alone. I'm not a mastermind, but it all just...worked out!"

Jade laughed. "Kind of. Aunt Sandy has never really struck me as someone who would...I don't know."

"Someone who would what?"

Jade shrugged. "I guess – someone who would pine after their high school sweetheart? Or pine after anyone at all. She doesn't seem like she needs anything, she's so...independent. Strong. And smart."

"While she *is* all of those things," Margie said, rinsing off the last plate, "she's also much more complicated than that."

"Oh great. All the more reason that she might be mad at us!"

Margie waved a hand. "Don't worry honey. She's not going to be mad at *you*. She's not going to be mad at all! Your Aunt Sandy – you're right about some of those things, and she's a very...intense person. When she sets her mind to something, nothing can stop her. And that's the same way she is in her relationships – she gives a hundred percent to people. Even when they don't deserve it."

"I thought she had a boyfriend?"

"No," Margie said with a sigh. "They broke up years ago. And he was – well excuse me, but he was a dud. He didn't deserve her. She's a great surgeon because she gives a hundred percent of herself to her patients, and she doesn't expect anything back from them. It's a good relationship, it works for her. That's how she is with everyone. It's the same with the residents that she trains. You know that she won the preceptor of the year award, right?"

"Oh yeah! I remember you telling me about that."

"She's an incredible woman. And it's hard to find a man who deserves her, or who will give a hundred percent effort into a relationship like she does."

Margie took a peek at her phone – maybe Sandy had sent a text message?

But no – there was nothing. What if she really *was* mad at her? That would make the visit a bit awkward.

Jade poured herself a cup of coffee. "And we just happened to find the right guy in the culinary section of the paper?"

Margie laughed. "I never said that. But he *really* loved her. And she *really* loved him. They were so young, though...I never understood why she broke up with him. She just made up her mind and that was the end of it."

"Maybe she had her reasons, Mom!" Jade rubbed her forehead. "What if she left the island because she was so upset?"

Margie settled in next to her with a coffee mug. "No, your aunt is not a hot head. And besides, we're sisters, she'd at least come and yell at me first if she was really angry."

Jade grunted but said nothing else.

"Don't get so worked up. It's okay. And I had to do something! Do you know what she said to me? After she found out that she had to take time off from work?"

"What?"

"Well, she sounded so down on herself and I was trying to convince her to come here and visit. I told her how wonderful moving here has been, and how I've gotten to spend so much time with you, and how I've fallen in love again."

"Aw, Mom!"

"And she said she's happy for me, but not everyone is lucky enough to find love. And she said that she's accepted that she's just not cut out for it, and she's okay with that."

"Oh..." Jade sat, staring into her coffee.

Margie frowned. Maybe she shouldn't have said that. Jade didn't talk much about her own recent divorce, and she didn't need to get those kinds of ideas in her head – that some people were simply not cut out for love.

"She's wrong, of course," Margie added. "She's just given up – and she's gotten away with that for a long time. But not anymore – not if I have anything to do with it."

Just then, the front door opened and Margie and Jade both froze. Margie felt panicked for a moment, trying to think of something to say – *anything* so that it wouldn't look like they had just been talking about Sandy.

Luckily Jade was a bit more quick thinking and called out, "Aunt Sandy, is that you?"

"It is!" She strolled into the kitchen, cheeks flushed and rosy. There was even a bit of sweat on her forehead despite it being quite chilly outside.

"We were starting to get worried about you," said Jade. "How far did you walk?"

"I have no idea!" replied Sandy. "But it was wonderful. So peaceful, so quiet. I found a spot for myself at the edge of the water and just sat for a while. What a view!"

"Good!" Margie clasped her hands together. "Can I get you some water? Orange juice? Oh – I made coffee too. And breakfast, when you're ready for it."

Sandy laughed. "That is some remarkable service, thank you. I hope I didn't wake you up this morning?"

Margie shook her head. "Absolutely not. I didn't even hear you sneak out. I wish you would've taken the car. Just so you know, I keep the keys in my purse and you can take them whenever you like."

"That's all right – and I didn't mean to hold up your breakfast."

"You came just in time," Jade said. She cleared her throat before adding, "Did you have a nice evening?"

Sandy accepted the glass of water that Margie handed her. "Oh yes, it was lovely. I went to that restaurant where they'd turned the entire menu into a Christmas theme."

"Did you see Santa?" Jade asked.

"Eventually." Sandy took a big swig of water. "But then it got so crowded that we had to leave."

Margie smiled. "Oh, where did you and Jack go then?"

"I was tired, so Jack offered to drop me off back here. Sorry that I missed you both. And Margie?"

Margie flashed a smile. "Yes?"

"That was a nice try with him, but it's not going to work. Though I do admire your effort."

"See Jade?" Margie said, handing Sandy a mug of coffee. "Your aunt didn't get so angry at me that she left the island."

Sandy threw her head back and laughed. "What?!"

"I didn't say that I thought you left," said Jade. "I was just, you know...concerned. And I want you to know that I had nothing to do with it, Aunt Sandy."

Sandy patted her on the shoulder. "Believe me, I never suspected you. I know what my sister is like. In fact, I've known her for her whole life."

"It's very good that you're not mad, and now we can move on to breakfast." Margie made a few cuts in the quiche.

"No, I'm not mad. But how do I put this? It's like – well, almost like I got a Christmas gift that I didn't want. And I don't mean to be rude and try to return it, but I never asked for it, you know?"

"Hm, can't say that's ever happened to me," Margie replied. "What would you say if there was an old-fashioned Christmas market in town and that present that you didn't like happened to be there, too?"

Sandy gave her a puzzled look. "What? Did you invite him without telling me?"

"It's the main event this weekend, Sandy! I can't tell the man not to attend all of the best Christmas activities. And yes, maybe I told him that he might get some ideas for party appetizers there. And that we were going to be there."

Sandy set her coffee down. "Of course. Hard to avoid someone on such a small island, isn't it?"

Jade giggled.

"That's the spirit!" Margie replied, serving her a slice of quiche. "You'll get to meet Hank too!"

"Yeah, about him," Sandy said. "Last night you went looking for Hank before you completely disappeared. Did you get... lost? Or does he not exist?"

"He does exist, and you're going to *love* him."

Sandy laughed and Margie shooed them into the dining room.

Maybe Margie *had* meddled a bit – but it certainly didn't seem like Sandy minded all that much.

It was a start. And maybe this beautiful island could help Sandy find hope – just as it had for Margie.

Chapter 5

It was hard for Sandy to resist eating too much at breakfast – the quiche that Margie made was a lovely mix of mushrooms, spinach and some kind of delicate cheese. She wanted to save some room for whatever creations were at the Christmas market, though, so she did the best she could to not overstuff herself.

She took a quick shower before joining Margie and Jade for the trip to Friday Harbor for the market. Margie chattered on, talking about the history of different sites and pointing out some of her neighbors' homes as they drove by.

Jade was quiet, which wasn't unusual, but Sandy wondered if she was still upset about the events of the morning. She made a mental note to find a time to talk to Jade and reassure her that she wasn't angry about the whole Jack situation.

Sandy rarely even got angry – she worked well under stress and could control her emotions. Which, come to think of it, only made it more embarrassing that she had snapped at her patient's mother.

She closed her eyes – *what* had gotten into her? Hopefully this get away would give her enough time to reflect on her actions.

But now she couldn't stop thinking about it – was this going to be her new thing? Was she losing her edge? Letting things get to her – like her anxiety on the flight in?

Or maybe she was tired and it was just a transient thing. A momentary lapse in judgment. But Sandy didn't like that excuse – just because she was human didn't mean she had to show it.

Thankfully, Sandy didn't have long to ruminate on it because they soon got into town. The first thing she noticed was the loud and cheerful Christmas music that enveloped the entire block. There was a band, dressed as elves, outside of the building playing a wonderful rendition of "Rockin' Around the Christmas Tree."

The area was crowded and Sandy saw delightful things everywhere she looked. There was music, food, and smiles all around. Even Santa had a new job today – he rode atop a tractor, dressed in his customary red suit, shouting in jolly tones to the children that he was pulling along in a hayride.

Outside of the building, there was a row of tents and a heavenly smell drifting toward them.

"What *is* that?" asked Sandy.

Jade squinted. "Looks like someone is selling roasted chestnuts. Would you like some?"

"I would love some. I have a feeling I'm not going to get very far before I'm stuffed."

Margie laughed. "Don't worry – they'll be here tomorrow too."

"Perfect."

They slowly moved past the various stalls, with Margie stopping to talk every few feet, seemingly knowing everyone.

"If I didn't know any better," Sandy said to Jade in a low voice, "I'd say that my sister was the mayor of San Juan Island."

Jade laughed. "Sometimes it feels like that. She's made a lot of friends."

Margie was always good at making friends, and Sandy was glad that her ex-husband Jeff was no longer holding her back. She was a bit nervous that Margie's new boyfriend – no, her fiancé – might not be a worthy choice. But from everything Margie said about him, he seemed almost too good to be true.

She didn't have to wait much longer to meet him – about twenty minutes into their browsing of some stunning island-made jewelry, the much-anticipated Hank showed up.

Sandy spotted him first – it was easy to do, as the tall, burly police chief tried to sneak up on Margie. Amazingly, she didn't see him because she was completely engrossed in a conversation with the jewelry designer.

He crept up slowly, shot a wink at Jade, and was just behind Margie when he yelled a very loud, "Boo!"

Margie reacted immediately with a stupendous jump and scream. When she turned around and saw that it was him, she burst into laughter and planted a kiss on his cheek.

"I should've known you'd do something like that."

"I couldn't resist," he said, beaming.

"Hank, I'd like you to meet my sister, Dr. Sandra Randall."

He stuck out his hand. "It's very nice to meet you, doctor."

Sandy had to resist laughing – Margie never missed an opportunity to gush about her being a doctor. Even when she sent a birthday card, she always addressed it to Dr. Sandra Randall. Sometimes she'd even add something on top like, "the distinguished Dr. Sandra Randall," or, "the honorable Dr. Sandra Randall."

Sandy shook his hand. "It's very nice to meet you too, Hank. I've heard so much about you. And please, call me Sandy."

They meandered into the building, chatting and stopping every few feet to browse. Hank introduced Sandy to a local farmer, and they got to hear a bit of history about the farm.

Sandy was impressed by the offerings – they had a huge variety of island-made biscotti, jams, and mustards. During the warmer months, they also had a constant supply of fresh fruits and vegetables. For Christmas, they'd put together some very pretty gift boxes that Sandy decided would be perfect to share with her coworkers back home.

Hank continued pointing out different stalls and introduced her to at least half a dozen people. It became obvious that Margie must have gotten a nice introduction to the community through Hank.

Sandy enjoyed his tour – and she enjoyed watching her sister with him. They were quite lovey-dovey. And she found herself quite at ease with him – he had a gruff sort of charm that struck her immediately.

It really seemed like Margie had found – no, created – the perfect home.

After meeting a local lavender farmer, Sandy excused herself to stand in line for some hot cider. She was in a bit of a daydream when a familiar voice snapped her out of it.

"Fancy seeing you here."

She turned around and saw that Jack was planted directly behind her.

"Right back at you."

"I'm glad that the eggnog from yesterday didn't put you off from all holiday drinks."

Sandy shook her head. "Not at all. Did you see how many flavors of hot cocoa they were selling out front?"

Jack raised his eyebrows. "I didn't. But I don't think that I can resist. Keep me away from the table – I think I had enough hot cocoa yesterday to last for the season."

It was Sandy's turn to order, so she stepped forward and asked for two medium hot ciders – one for her, and one for Jack.

"That was very smooth," he said. "And very inconvenient. I was planning to buy *you* some cider so I could ask you for a favor."

She turned away from him to pay the cashier. "What kind of favor?"

"Nothing big – I just wanted to see if you were interested in being involved with some of the menu preparation for your sister's party."

Sandy accepted the two cups of cider and handed one to Jack. "I feel like this is a good time to tell you that I'm a terrible cook."

"That's perfect – you wouldn't have to cook anything. Just offer some opinions – and some taste testing."

She took a sip of cider. "I'll think about it."

"Fair enough."

Sandy motioned to the bag he was holding. "Looks like you've already gotten a few things?"

He nodded, opening the bag. "Yeah, there's all kinds of great stuff here. Check this out – a pizza cutter with a wooden whale tail handle."

Sandy laughed. "It's very pretty. I didn't know you liked whales."

He nodded. "I didn't either. But I stopped into the whale museum this morning and learned about the killer whale pods that live around the islands."

"Oh neat! Are they around this time of year?"

"Unfortunately, most of them are not. There are some transient whale pods that show up sometimes, but they aren't as predictable as the resident pods. Those come by mainly in the summer, chasing the salmon. I talked to the lady at the museum and she said that there hasn't been a sighting of any of them recently."

"Too bad. I've gone on some really nice whale watching tours out in Boston. What else you do have in there?"

"I've got some sea salt...salted caramels...and some locally roasted coffee. That's all for Helen – I think she'd really like visiting here so this will be my first step in trying to convince her."

"Convince, or bribe?" Sandy said with a smile.

"Is there really a difference?"

When they were younger, Sandy thought that Jack wasn't cut out for family life – that he was too rebellious, too wild. But it turned out she was very wrong and last night, when she saw the hundreds of pictures of his daughter he had on his phone, she was quite touched.

"That'll be nice," she said. "So yesterday you said that you're going to move out to the east coast to be closer to her. Do you already have a new restaurant in the works?"

He let out a sigh. "No. I honestly have no idea what I'm doing. When the offer came in to buy the restaurant in Seattle, initially I thought I would say no. But it was too good to pass up – and perfect timing. But now...I don't know what to do with myself. I don't know the market out there, I don't have any contacts. It might be really foolish to start a new venture."

"I trust that you'll figure it out. You just need to decide what you want and go for it. Make a plan. Like you did with the first place."

He paused. "Make a plan..."

"Yeah – you know, make a list. Make a bunch of lists. And make a one year plan, a five year plan, and a ten year plan. Actually write them out. Then figure out what your goals need to be, and start working toward them. It seems like you're pretty good at that."

He smiled. "Don't make me blush. But that's a great idea – I don't know why I've never thought of that before."

"You're welcome," she said.

Without missing a beat, he said, "My one week plan is to get you to be my taste-tester."

Sandy laughed and rolled her eyes. "Uh huh."

"What could I do to get you – no, us – closer to that goal?"

She looked around, annoyed that she couldn't spot Margie anywhere. Where could they have gone?

Oh – their disappearance was probably by design. Again.

"Did you ever learn to make your mom's baklava?" Sandy asked.

A smile spread across his face. "You bet! I'll get started on a tray today. As you can see, I'm not above trying to bribe you."

Sandy smiled at him. She was never one to pass up baklava, and she'd never found one to match the one that Jack's mom made when they were growing up.

Also, this party seemed like it might be important for Margie's business. It couldn't hurt for Sandy to get a little involved to do some quality control.

"Then you've got yourself a deal, chef."

Chapter 6

Somehow Jack convinced Sandy to spend a few hours with him each day leading up to the Christmas cookie party. He wasn't sure how he did it – was Margie busy and Sandy grew bored of waiting around? Did she want an excuse to get out of the house? Or was she simply hungry?

Jack didn't really care *what* the reason was – he found himself pulling out all of the stops to keep her interested. His first move was to make an absurd amount of baklava, as promised. Then he sent her a recipe for a Christmas tree shaped cheese ball.

"What do you think?" He asked in the text message. "I'm hoping to find enough appetizers so that everything can be Christmas themed."

"You know I love a challenge," she responded.

And with that, Sandy was hooked. The next day when they met at a coffee shop to go over ideas, she showed up with almost twenty recipes. There was everything from strawberry Santa bites, to a corn dog wreath, to even an enormous Christmas tree-shaped puff pastry.

"Now I think that some of these might be pretty challenging," she said. "I'm not sure that you're up for it."

"Oh I'm up for it," he said, trying not to smile. "The question is if any of these things are any good. It would be a disservice to your sister if we didn't try making these recipes at least a few times before we decide on the menu."

Sandy tapped her chin. "You're right. That would be very irresponsible of you, and could possibly ruin my sister's business before it even has a chance to take off."

He nodded. "That would be very unfortunate indeed."

"Agreed. The thing is – I promised the girls that I would go on a wildlife tour with them today."

"That's not a problem. Just give me the recipes and I'll get all of the ingredients. And how about tomorrow you come over and we can make them?"

"*All* of them?"

He shrugged. "I have nothing else to do. Plus, cooking happens to be my favorite activity."

She studied him for a moment. "I don't know what my plans are tomorrow – I'm sure Margie has something in mind."

"That's fine. I'll be working all day. So whenever you have some free time – stop by."

Sandy appeared to be satisfied with this arrangement, and the next day around one o'clock, she showed up at his rental house. He'd gotten all of the ingredients and prepared a lot of the cold foods, but delayed making some of the hot items until she came. He wanted to make sure that she got the full experience, and that included him getting a chance to show off a little bit.

They spent the rest of the afternoon together, laughing and sampling the various recipes. His first attempt at the Santa shaped strawberries was a mess – he wanted to use his own recipe for the whipped cream, but it ended up being too soft.

The Santas melted, slowly and pitifully, in a scene that Sandy called "The Great Santa Massacre." They laughed so hard that they were both in tears, collecting the strawberry shaped bodies "off of the battlefield" to eat and start again.

And try as he might, his puff pastry Christmas tree never quite worked. After two failed attempts, Sandy postulated that perhaps pastries weren't his strong suit. He admitted that he didn't spend as much time baking as he liked, and that it might be a good idea to try some more recipes the next day.

Sandy was in agreement there. Jack enjoyed her company enormously, and the task of making these new foods was an engrossing challenge that he loved.

Still, he hoped to find *some* way to use one of his perfected recipes on the menu. That night while he was looking online, he found a recipe for a melted snowman potato soup.

The melted part was easy enough – he needed to cut olives for the eyes and mouths, and cut carrot wedges for the noses. For the soup itself, he planned to use his own recipe.

Sandy came over the next day and he proudly handed her a shallow mug filled with soup, the snowman's features slowly drifting apart.

Sandy laughed. "Oh my gosh! Look at his cute, sad little face. How could you do this to a poor snowman?"

As she laughed, the mug shook slightly, exacerbating the snowman's melted look. Her laughter was contagious and Jack found himself getting caught up as well.

"He wasn't like that a minute ago," he argued.

"He's melting so fast!" she said, wiping tears from her face.

"Then put him out of his misery," said Jack. "Please – I can't take it anymore, his nose is almost completely sideways."

Once she caught her breath, Sandy took a bite of the soup.

"Wow!" She had another spoonful. "That is *really* excellent. Where did you find this recipe?"

"The soup is mine, actually. It was a seasonal item in my restaurant – took me years to find the right blend of flavors. I got the idea for the melted snowman face online."

"You have to do this for the party! Even if it's just in little mugs – people can walk around with mugs, right?"

He nodded. "I'm sure they could. Do you think Margie would like it?"

"Margie would love it. I'm sure she's not expecting to get all of these very Christmasy foods, but she'll be delighted. When you hand her a mug of melted snowman, she'll just die of laughter. It'll be the talk of the island, I'm sure of it. And she can put it on her website."

"Well, whatever you say goes. Margie didn't give me much direction on what she wanted – so it's totally up to us."

"Perfect. We're going to knock this out of the park."

The day before the party, Sandy was busy helping Margie prepare everything in the barn, and Jack didn't get a chance to see her. It was just as well – he had a lot to prepare and cook.

Margie had a caterer's kitchen at the barn, but he preferred to use the kitchen in his rental for most things. The majority of the foods they settled on were easy finger foods that they could put out in batches and not have to worry about passing around, so the catering kitchen was useful for storage.

The one exception to their easy going appetizers was the soup – but that was worth it. Sandy loved it so much that Jack didn't mind doling out soup all night. He would make anything that she wanted him to make as long as he could keep talking to her and keep making her laugh.

He'd always regretted how their relationship ended, and now it felt like he was getting a second chance – and he was captivated getting to know the woman that Sandy became.

Somehow when he was with her, he wasn't worried about what he would be doing the next year, the next month, or even the next week. He only cared about the moment that he was in – he wanted to make his time with her count.

On Saturday, he got up early to make sure that everything was in order for the party. He wasn't used to working by himself, but he enjoyed it.

Margie stressed to him that she only wanted light appetizers and that she didn't expect a huge turnout. She also insisted that he find time to enjoy the party.

"And maybe," she said, "you'll find some time to ask Sandy to dance?"

He smiled. "I'll always have time for that."

Margie smiled approvingly but said nothing else. Instead, she rushed off to hang some fake snow, adding to the charming copious garland and Christmas lights.

Jack appreciated that she stopped even trying to hide what she was up to and was now openly advocating that he flirt with Sandy.

Once everything was set up, Jack went home and changed into clean clothes. Though Margie encouraged him to wear something festive, he didn't have much to work with. He hadn't brought anything Christmasy with him, so a Santa hat from the local shop would have to do.

He got back in the barn quickly and made sure that everything was in order – particularly that the soup was heated and ready to be served, along with all of the little garnishes for the snowmen faces.

Now, even as guests started coming in and marveling at the splendor of the party, Sandy was nowhere to be seen. He wondered if she'd find a way to avoid him for the entire day. He checked in with Margie, who said that Sandy was busy dealing with some work issues – apparently, she'd gotten a call from one of her residents asking for help on a patient case. Sandy had been locked away in her room working on it for some time.

Jack liked that about her – no, he *loved* that about her. There were no half measures with Sandy. She always gave whatever she was doing her full attention. It was something he'd always admired about her, even when they were growing up.

An hour into the party, Sandy was still nowhere to be seen. Jack kept busy with the appetizers and helped direct people to the contest table – it was genuinely surprising how many people were prepared to enter the cookie contest. It seemed like everyone knew each other, and they were actually excited to be a part of it. It was sweet – very different from what he was used to living in the city.

Margie had put together a number of different categories for winners, too – there was one for most creative, best decoration, best taste, and of course, best in show. Every category also had a junior category for kids who wanted to enter.

On top of that, there was a station for younger kids where they could decorate cookies. These were lovingly baked by Margie herself, which Jack found quite impressive. The woman was a baking machine. He made a mental note to ask her if she had any puff pastry tricks.

Jack was able to keep himself busy bouncing around between the tables and ensuring that there was enough hot cider and hot cocoa available at the two self-serve stations. The atmosphere was quite relaxed, and after a few rounds he realized that there was nothing else he could do.

He was in a prime position to enjoy the party – the only issue being that Sandy was still missing. He casually checked around for her as he did some spot checks on the appetizer platters – and while the barn was big, it wasn't *that* big. There was nowhere for her to hide, really. Was it possible she was skipping out? Or had to head back home for some emergency?

Margie was busy chatting with people and laughing. Jade was occupied with the table of children, trying her best to guide icing-covered fingers and clean up spills of sprinkles.

No – Sandy wouldn't just leave without saying goodbye. Would she?

Jack was about to send her a text message when he spotted her out of the corner of his eye. It was almost as if she'd read his mind.

He stood up straight, straining to get a clearer view of her as she stepped into the barn. She was dressed from head to toe in a forest green elf costume – complete with a jingle bell tipped hat, merrily bouncing with her every move.

They made eye contact from across the room and she smiled.

It was like an arrow went through his heart.

Chapter 7

Sandy waved at Jack, then realized that a five year old girl spotted her from across the room and was furiously waving back. She walked over to her to ask her what she was up to.

Suddenly the girl became shy.

"It's okay, say hello to Santa's helper," the girl's mother said softly.

"I will have to tell Santa how well behaved you've been this year," Sandy said, squatting down.

A smile spread across the girl's face. "Thank you!" she yelled before running off.

Sandy stood up and surveyed the scene in front of her. The barn looked marvelous – Margie had outdone herself with the decorations, even going as far as to set up a beautiful, fully decorated, twelve foot Christmas tree in the corner.

The cookie contest table had a decent number of entrants, all laid out on individual plates and numbered with index cards. Sandy was glad that she skipped lunch – she would need to be hungry to judge the cookies fairly.

Margie was busy fussing around and Jade seemed to be trying to herd a group of children. Sandy had seen Jack long before he spotted her – he was much less fussy than Margie, checking on things in an easy and calm manner.

He looked nice – he didn't have an elaborate costume like Sandy did, but he looked clean in his button up shirt and over-sized red Santa hat. He looked...cute.

She studied him for a moment – he didn't seem to notice that she was watching. He was chatting in his easy way, going from table to table and making sure that everything was well stocked. There was a lot of him that was unchanged from when they were young – his humor, his ease with people. His hazel eyes...

That was perhaps the most jarring. When Sandy looked into his eyes, it was like being transported back in time. And she'd spent a lot of time with him for the past few days, looking into his eyes, laughing to the point of tears. She didn't *intend* for that to happen, but it just worked out that way.

It was easy to spend time with him; the hours melted away. She didn't have to try to be any certain way, or watch what she said or did – she felt relaxed. She didn't have to think too hard. Even though he didn't know all of the details of her life until now, he still knew her – the real her.

She walked over to Jack and said her hellos.

"I didn't know that Santa was loaning us one of his helpers today," he commented.

Sandy made a small curtsy. "Yes, today I'm at Margie's service. Santa said that it was of the utmost importance to increase the holiday cheer in this barn."

He smiled. "You're doing a great job."

"Thanks."

"Where did you get this? Did I miss the Christmas shop in town?"

She looked down at herself. She really liked this particular outfit – from the little hat, to the matching green tights, and even the loud bells on her shoes. "No. I got it a few years ago, actually. Every Christmas, Santa comes to visit the kids in our hospital. I got it so that I could tag along and pretend to be one of his helpers."

"That's...incredibly sweet."

"Don't start getting all mushy on me," she said, hands on her hips. "Have you shown Margie the soup yet?"

He shook his head. "No – I wanted to wait for you. Shall we?"

"Please!"

She followed him and watched as he carefully put together a melted snowman, first pouring the soup into a mug, then delicately placing the garnishes for the face. He flashed her a smile before walking over to Margie and tapping her on the shoulder.

"Excuse me for interrupting, but I need your final approval on the appetizers today."

Margie turned around, a smile on her face. "Everything has just been wonderful Jack!"

"There's one more thing that you haven't tried," Sandy added.

Margie gave her a puzzled look and accepted the mug from Jack. "What's this? Mulled cider?"

Sandy shook her head and Margie took a look into the mug.

"Oh my goodness – what is this!"

"Melted snowman soup," said Sandy. "Straight from the North Pole."

Margie threw her head back and laughed. "This is unbelievable! Jack, I had no idea you were so talented – thank you."

Sandy felt oddly proud – she sort of had a hand in it, but not really. It was all Jack.

Within moments, he was bombarded with requests for soup. He dutifully went over to the kettle so that he could dole out mug after mug. Sandy helped him for a while before deciding that she couldn't resist taking a break and getting a mug for herself.

She stepped away to enjoy it for a moment; it was just as good as she remembered. She was savoring her last spoonful when Margie pulled her into a conversation and introduced her to two of her friends.

One lady, Barb, was the president of the small business association on the island and Sandy got the impression that she was somewhat important to Margie's success.

"Hey, I'll tell you what – I was happy to have Margie spruce this barn up," said Barb. "She's done a great job and it gives people more reason to come to the island."

The other woman, Linda, agreed. "Oh yes, it's adorable! I'm sure we'll be seeing a lot of big weddings coming through next year."

"Do you also run a business?" asked Sandy.

Linda shook her head. "Oh goodness no – I actually just retired. I was a dental hygienist for thirty years."

"How interesting." Sandy took a step closer to her. She'd initially thought they were probably about the same age, but now, she decided that Linda was perhaps a little older. "What's it like being retired? I've heard so many different reports."

Linda sighed. "Oh you know – at first it's wonderful. All that free time! No getting up early, no rushing around. But I firmly believe that if you don't stay active, your mind will wither away."

"I'm never going to retire," said Barb. "They'll find me at my desk one day – dead!"

They all laughed. Sandy was unsure about her own retire-ment. It wasn't truly something she was interested in. Maybe she would cut back on her hours one day? Or do more teach-ing?

But to leave medicine entirely...she would only do that if it was unsafe for her to continue practicing. There was nothing she wanted to retire to – she worked towards being a surgeon for almost sixteen years. It was all she'd ever really wanted.

"So what do you do to stay busy?" asked Sandy. "Have you gotten a lot of new hobbies?"

"Oh yes!" said Linda. "I've tried just about everything. The quilting didn't work out – I think I've gone too far in my life *without* quilting to pick it up now. But I've been able to cook more, which is nice. I started a garden and ended up with an overabundance of green beans, so *then* I had to learn canning... you know, there's been a real domino effect of hobbies."

"Sounds awful," Barb said.

Linda laughed and lightly tapped Barb on the shoulder. "No, it's great! I've even started painting again. I hadn't painted in years."

"Really?" Sandy said. "Do you have any pictures of your work?"

"I do," Linda said, pulling her phone from her purse. "Mostly it's things like this..."

She scrolled through some pictures on her phone – mainly there were paintings of animals, a few chickens and horses. There was a lot of color in the paintings, and they looked lively – happy, even. Sandy wasn't well versed in art, but the paint-ings gave her a distinct feeling of joy.

"Linda, these are *really* beautiful," Sandy said.

"Thank you! I guess I need to stick with painting. I think I picked up too many things all at once – my goal for this upcoming year is to focus a bit more."

Sandy smiled. "Well it sounds like you've been pretty adventurous."

"I'd like to travel more," she continued. "But my husband still works. That's probably for the better, though – I don't think he would like being retired. But maybe we can take a nice trip somewhere together. Who knows, the world is our oyster!"

Sandy was happy to keep chatting, but Margie reappeared and told her and Barb that all of the entries were in for the cookie contest and that they needed to start their rounds.

"I've been waiting for this all day," Barb said. "Let's go Mrs. Claus."

Sandy waved her ahead. "After you."

Margie provided them each with a clipboard so that they could take notes and keep track of their favorites. At the end of their taste tests, they needed to give Margie their scorecards so she could tally up the votes.

As they were sampling the first cookies, Jack stopped over with two mugs of milk. "I thought this might be an important tool in helping with your responsibilities."

Sandy accepted a mug from him. "Thank you Jack – this is exactly what I needed."

She took a sip of the milk just as she heard something fall to the ground. Sandy looked over to Barb and saw that her right arm hung limp at her side, the cup shattered on the floor in a puddle of milk.

"Barb – are you okay?" asked Sandy.

Barb didn't respond – she didn't even look at Sandy.

Jack and Sandy locked eyes for a moment before Sandy took a step forward. "Barb? Barb, can you hear me?"

Still no response. Sandy could see the distinct change in Barb's face – one side of her mouth looked downturned.

"Jack – I need you to call 911. Now."

"You got it."

Sandy took Barb by the arm and gently tried to guide her to a chair – she didn't want her to fall and hit her head, adding to the chaos of the situation.

She was able to get Barb to a table nearby and settled her into her seat. Barb still wasn't able to say anything – it seemed like she was trying to, but she was speaking quietly and not making any sense.

Sandy stayed with her, talking to her continuously and trying to get her to respond. After a few moments, Margie joined her.

"What's going on? What's wrong?"

Sandy could hear the panic in her voice.

"I'm not sure," she said slowly. "One minute we were eating cookies and chatting, and the next minute she was like this. Does she have anyone here? Her husband?"

"He didn't come!" Margie said, her volume rising.

"It's okay, don't panic. Jack called an ambulance, and I'll go to the hospital with her."

"Sandy what's happening? Is she going to be okay?"

"Don't worry, we're going to get her to the hospital. Okay?"

Margie nodded, her face pale.

The paramedics arrived quickly and evaluated Barb. Within minutes, Sandy was in the back of the ambulance with her, continuing to provide as much information as she could.

She managed to grab Barb's purse on the way out and brought it with her. She tried calling Barb's husband using her cell phone, but he didn't answer. Luckily, she was able to find a medication list in Barb's wallet and gave that to the paramedics.

About five minutes into their ride to the hospital, Barb started to come to.

"What's going on? Why am I stuck in here?"

Sandy backed off and allowed the paramedics to evaluate the now cantankerous Barb. She passed their questioning with flying colors and insisted that she needed to be dropped off at home.

Sandy had to bite her lip to stop herself from laughing. She was relieved to see that Barb recovered, but she also insisted on a trip to the hospital.

"But I'm fine now!" said Barb. "Nothing is wrong with me."

Sandy kept her tone even. "But something was very wrong with you back at the party. Come on – it won't take long. Let the doctor check you out and run some scans."

Barb let out a dramatic sigh. "This is ridiculous."

"I'm glad you feel better now, but we need to find out what happened."

"I changed my mind," Barb said. "I don't think you're Mrs. Claus anymore. You're one of the seven dwarves. Grumpy! You're Grumpy!"

Now Sandy couldn't help but laugh. If anyone was Grumpy, it was Barb.

She waited a moment until Barb stopped talking. "Are you ready to go in now?"

"Fine – but tell Margie that I want my cookies sent here."

"I can have that arranged. Now let's get inside."

Chapter 8

Margie did what she could to keep the party running, but she was worried sick about Barb. Maybe there really was something wrong at the barn that was making people ill? Or maybe – heaven forbid – something was wrong with the food?

But no, that didn't make sense – food poisoning didn't strike suddenly like that. What was going on?

Margie didn't have to wait too long for an answer; after about forty minutes, Sandy called her from the hospital.

"It seems that Barb has recovered – but they're running some tests."

"Oh thank goodness!" Margie said. "I've been so worried."

"Another thing – to get her to agree to come inside, I had to make a deal with her."

"Oh?"

Sandy laughed. "She demanded that her cookies be brought here so she can continue sampling."

Margie closed her eyes. What a demand. "You're kidding! Do you think that's a good idea? What if the cookies made her sick?"

"I think that's very unlikely," said Sandy. "It could have been a number of things, but probably not the food. Is anyone else suddenly falling ill?"

Margie paused and looked around. The music was still playing, kids were running around – everyone seemed to be back to enjoying the festivities. "No. No one else is ill...yet."

"Don't worry Margie – they'll figure out what happened. And Barb is fine. All is well."

Margie wasn't sure about that, but she was glad that Barb had at least recovered. "Should I pack up some cookies then and drive them over?"

"Actually, I don't think you need to trouble yourself. Hank got wind of the commotion and stopped by to check on everything."

Margie heard a muffled, "Hey honey!" in the background.

She smiled. "And all this time I thought he was working."

"He *is* working," said Sandy. "But now, apparently, he can make it part of his official duties to pick up those cookies for Barb. He said he'll stop by now."

Margie laughed. "That's perfect."

She prepared a container of cookies for Barb, carefully labeling each one so that she could still record her scores. Hank got to the barn just as she was finishing up; Margie was quite pleased that he found an excuse to stop by.

"You've done it again," he said, surveying the barn. "This is a remarkable testament to your decorating skills and top-notch holiday cheer."

"Thank you honey," she said with a sigh. "Though I feel like things are falling apart."

He wrapped her in a bear hug. "Oh come on, that doesn't sound like my positive ray of sunshine."

She wasn't able to move even an inch. She let out a huff. "Maybe I need to shut this whole operation down before anyone else gets sick."

He squeezed tighter. "Now, now. You don't mean that. Everything is fine, look at all of these smiling faces! Everyone's happy. Don't worry so much, okay?"

Margie stopped trying to squirm away and released the tension in her body. It felt nice to rest her weight on him. "Okay."

He kissed her on the forehead and accepted the cookies. "I have to run, but I'll bring Sandy back and then we can both cheer you up."

"That sounds nice," Margie said with a faint smile.

As promised, he returned with Sandy about an hour later. Unfortunately, they didn't have any news on Barb's condition. She seemed to be back to normal, but the doctor was able to convince Barb to spend the night in the hospital for observation.

Sandy said it could have been a number of things – Bell's palsy, a mini stroke, Lyme disease, or even something serious like a tumor.

That one made Margie gasp.

"I don't think it's anything like that," Sandy assured her. "Her bloodwork was wonderfully boring. And it was so sudden – much more likely to be one of the other reasons."

Margie frowned. "It was so frightening. But you were so calm! How did you stay so calm?"

"That's my thing," Sandy said with a smile. "And we know that it wasn't the cookies or the food or something here at the barn – so don't worry about that, okay?"

Margie found it hard not to worry, but she managed to get through tallying up the scores and giving out the awards for the cookie contest.

She was relieved when the party was finally over. She'd been so excited to bring people together and cover the barn in Christmas decorations, but it had turned into a nightmare. Margie went to bed early that night, exhausted.

The next morning, she woke up early to give Hank a ride to the airport. He was flying to London to join his daughter for Christmas. Margie would miss him, but she was happy that he was able to make the trip and spend some time with her.

When she got back from dropping him off, she was surprised to see that Sandy arranged some sort of breakfast spread.

"Did you make this?" she asked, her eyes darting between the pile of pastries and plate of sliced cheese.

Sandy laughed. "Of course not! But I found these places on my morning walk so I picked up a few things along the way. I got some pastries from a bakery down the road, picked up this fruit at the grocery store, and I even managed to find some good looking cheese. What do you think?"

Margie smiled. "I think this is very considerate of you and I love you."

Sandy smiled and handed Margie a mug of coffee. They sat down to enjoy breakfast when Margie heard her phone go off.

"Let me just check who that is. I'm hoping that it's not Hank with his flight canceled or something."

"Take your time." Sandy loaded a plate with pastries and fruit.

Margie grabbed her phone out of her purse and saw that it was a text message.

She gasped.

Sandy looked up. "What's wrong?"

"It's Linda."

"Oh – from the party?"

Margie nodded. "She wrote, 'Have you heard any more from Barb? I'm not feeling so well...headed to the hospital now.' "

Sandy set her danish onto her plate. "Well...that's not good."

Chapter 9

"Not good? It's terrible!" Margie said, both hands on her face.

"It doesn't mean that it has anything to do with you or the barn," Sandy said gently.

Margie started pacing. "This is the *third* person who's gotten sick after coming to a party here."

"Third?"

"Yes! It all started with Edgar when he said that the water made him sick, and – "

"Oh him?" Sandy shook her head. "I'm willing to bet he drank too much wine and needed to find something to blame to save face with his coworkers."

"Who knows how many more people are sick and haven't told me yet? What if they're just flooding the hospital!"

Oh boy. The panic train had already left the station. "Margie, sit down. Relax. It's fine! Ask Linda what's wrong. She could be having a heart attack for all we know."

"I messaged her, but she hasn't answered. And she asked about Barb, so she must think it's related!"

"Well, have you heard from Barb today?"

Margie frowned. "No. Do you think she's okay?"

"Yes, I think she's fine." Sandy stood so she be closer to her sister – maybe a reassuring touch on the shoulder would help. "Why don't you call her? And then we can tell Linda how she's doing."

"I don't want to bother her," Margie said. "Oh my gosh – I'm supposed to catch the ferry to Anacortes in thirty minutes. I have a meeting with a vendor on the mainland, but maybe I should cancel so I can…"

Sandy put up a hand. "No, don't cancel. Don't panic. How about I talk to Barb, and then I can stop by the hospital and see what's going on with Linda?"

"Are you sure? I don't want to ruin your day."

Sandy nodded. "I'm sure. And I would have a much worse day if I knew that you were worrying about all of this."

Margie stood, unmoved, staring into space.

After a moment, Sandy prompted her again. "Really – it'll be fine. Let me check into it. I'm sure that Linda is just on high alert after seeing Barb get hauled away in an ambulance."

"You might be right. How will you get there? I have to take the car on the ferry with me."

"Oh, right." Sandy crossed her arms. Maybe she could get a reliable taxi for the day? Or… "Is Jade around?"

Margie shook her head. "No – she had to meet with her lawyer about the divorce."

"Ah."

Margie looked up at her, a smile forming. "But I have an idea."

"What?"

"Jack! I'm sure he doesn't have anything to do."

"How can you be so sure?" Sandy said. "And now I'm wondering – is Linda *really* going to the hospital, or is this another part of your elaborate scheme?"

"Of course not! I would never make something up like that."

"Fair enough. Well…I guess I don't have a lot of other options. Unless you have a bicycle around here or something?"

Margie shook her head. "What on earth would I do with a bicycle?"

"All right – I'll give him a call. Sit down and eat something, okay?"

Margie nodded and took a seat, but her eyes were focused off in the distance.

Sandy stepped into her room before calling Jack.

"Hey stranger!" he said as soon as he picked up.

"Hey Jack, how're you doing today?"

"I'm doing pretty well, and yourself?"

She let out a sigh. "I'm doing fine, but Margie got some unsettling news. Apparently, another woman who was at the party yesterday isn't feeling well."

"Oh – what kind of unwell?"

"I'm not sure – we haven't been able to get any answers. And we haven't heard back from Barb, so naturally, Margie is certain that it had something to do with her party."

"Well that's not good."

She continued. "I don't believe that's the case, though. I was thinking that I would stop over at the hospital and feel things out."

"That's a good idea."

She closed her eyes. "And I was hoping that you could maybe give me a ride? If you're not busy."

"I'm not busy at all! I would be honored. When do you want me?"

Sandy peeked her head out of the door and saw that Margie was still sitting there, frozen. "Whenever you're ready, I'm ready."

"Okay, I'll leave now. See you soon."

"Thanks Jack. See you."

Sandy gave Margie the update and managed to convince her to eat at least half of a danish. She also got both Barb and Linda's phone numbers from Margie so that she could get in contact with them.

Margie then insisted on getting Jack's phone number – something Sandy had a feeling that she would regret, but she obliged.

"You have to promise me that you won't be freaking out all day," said Sandy.

Margie turned toward her. "I'll make no such promise. Especially if my Christmas party is the source of all major disease on San Juan Island."

Sandy groaned. "Don't be so dramatic. We don't know anything yet – so don't make things up in your head."

"I'll try," Margie said.

Jack arrived just as Margie was getting things ready to leave for the ferry. Sandy gave her a hug and told her not to worry.

Jack was waiting at the front door.

"This is a beautiful house," he said. "I didn't get a chance to really talk to you about it yesterday."

Sandy nodded. "It is – and Margie has done a lot with it. Are you ready to go?"

"Of course. My only regret is that I don't have my motorcycle from my school days so that you could ride in style."

"After seeing the kind of injuries that happen on motorcycles, I would *never* get on a motorcycle again. So you're safe there."

"Oh, right." He stepped aside and dramatically swooped a hand over the car. "Which is why I have this very safe midsize sedan to drive you around in."

"Thank you." She got into the passenger seat and buckled her seat belt.

He buckled his own seat belt and they started the trip to the hospital. Sandy watched him for a moment – he did everything so carefully. From putting the car in reverse, to checking the road, to even driving the speed limit.

He drove so responsibly; it was quite different from the young man that she remembered. Life had certainly changed him – just as it had changed her.

"So we're pretty certain that I poisoned everyone yesterday, right?" he asked, shooting her a smile.

That made her laugh. "Of course not. Barb certainly didn't react to the food. If I could just get a hold of her, I could find out what happened. And I have no idea what happened to Linda. I sent her a text message but she hasn't answered yet."

"Maybe I shouldn't have put so much gold dust in the soup. Could that lead to heavy metal poisoning?"

She turned to him. "Wait – why do you put gold dust in the soup?"

He laughed. "I'm kidding. I didn't put any metal in the soup. Sorry – is it too soon to joke about that?"

"Oh, no, sorry." She let out a little laugh. "I'm just trying to think of anything that could make people ill."

"You're right – I'll try to keep the joking to a minimum."

"No, that's fine. As long as you're not panicking like Margie, then we're good. She was really...jumping to conclusions."

"Understandable."

Sandy frowned. "Panicking doesn't help, though. It prevents you from thinking clearly."

"Well," he said, slowly taking a turn, "I believe you. But I also remember a time when you weren't so good at keeping your cool."

Sandy looked out of the window so he wouldn't see that she was smiling. "I don't know what you're talking about."

"Think back. Way back. Biology lab in the eleventh grade."

Sandy narrowed her eyes. "I have a vague memory of this."

"The blacktop desks? The broken glassware? And the infuriating Mrs. Johnson?"

Sandy groaned. "Yes. She *hated* me!"

"She did seem to particularly dislike you," he said with a laugh. "Now, do you remember some of the dissections we had to do?"

Sandy shook her head. "Honestly I don't. Did I block this out?"

"There was a worm...a frog...and a pig."

"Oh my gosh," she said, slapping her forehead. "Yes, that pig! I almost got suspended because of that pig."

"No, you almost got suspended because you weren't able to remove the pig's brain, like instructed, and you accused Mrs. Johnson of giving you dull scissors."

"I maintain that she did."

"And *then* you went on a rant about how wasteful it was for everyone to have their own pig when you didn't even have the tools to properly dissect them..."

The memory flashed in her mind and Sandy chuckled. "Okay, yes, it's all coming back to me."

"And the principal asked you not to disrupt class like that anymore and instead write your impassioned speeches in the form of a paper, which he promised to read."

"You have a very good memory, Jack."

He shrugged. "For some things."

They got to the hospital and Sandy hesitated about what to do next – she hadn't gotten any texts and it was unlikely that Linda would be sitting out in the emergency room lobby, easily accessible.

It was also unlikely that the staff would let Sandy just waltz in and talk to her, either. She decided to try calling Linda.

No answer.

Hm. Only a moment later, though, her phone rang.

She cleared her throat. "Hi, this is Sandy."

A man's voice came through. "You're Margie's sister, right?"

"That's right."

"I'm Linda's husband, David." His voice cracked a bit when he said her name. "I'm with Linda at the hospital...she can't talk right now."

"Oh – I'm sorry, I didn't mean to bother – "

"She just – she just had to be intubated."

Sandy turned toward Jack with wide eyes. He mouthed a "what?" at her, but she turned away.

"I'm so sorry David."

"Linda said you're a doctor. Do you know what's going on?"

Sandy took a deep breath. "No, but I'm trying to figure it out. Are you in the hospital?"

"Yes."

She unbuckled her seat belt. "I'm coming in. I'll see you in a moment."

Chapter 10

She turned toward him. "Linda was just intubated."

"Uh – I *think* I know what that means but can you just remind me?"

"Yes, sorry. It means that she wasn't able to breathe on her own, so they had to put a tube down into her throat so she could breathe on a ventilator."

"Right. Wow – that's terrible."

Sandy nodded. "I'm going to go inside and talk to her husband – do you want to come, or...?"

"Of course!"

They walked into the emergency room lobby – there was only one person waiting. Jack assumed it must be Linda's husband. Sandy walked right up to him.

"David? Hi – I'm Sandy, Margie's sister."

He stood up quickly and reached to shake her hand. His skin was quite pale – especially his lips, which Jack found rather unsettling.

"Hi Sandy – thanks for coming. They just...well, I don't really know what's going on."

Sandy took a seat. "Can you tell me what happened? When did Linda's symptoms start?"

He sat next to her. "Well, I guess it was last night, really. I'm not sure if it was related, but she felt nauseous. She didn't throw up, but she just felt sick."

Maybe Jack's cooking *did* have something to do with it. That was his worst nightmare. He shot a look at Sandy, but she was focused on David.

"Okay. Was she able to sleep?"

David nodded. "Yeah, she thought it might be something to do with her new diet."

"What kind of diet?"

"She's just been trying to lose weight, so she's been fasting. She thought that maybe the nausea was just from the fasting. And maybe it was."

Sandy nodded. "Okay. How long does she fast?"

"She became a night owl since she retired, and she's been doing this really long fast where she only eats four hours a day. Between six and ten in the evening."

"Oh, wow."

Sandy paused and Jack realized that he was staring at her. Luckily, Sandy was completely focused on David and didn't seem to notice that Jack was even there. Everything she was doing, from her posture to the way she asked questions, made it clear that her full attention was on David.

She continued. "I was with her at the party yesterday – the Christmas party. Do you know if she ate anything there?"

"No. And the doctor here asked the same thing, but Linda said she was fasting. She didn't have a bite of anything." A faint smile spread across his face. "She has an iron will."

"It sure sounds like it," Sandy said, reaching out to rest her hand on top of his.

David sighed. "We had dinner together. At home last night. That's when she started feeling sick. And then this morning she woke up and she was dizzy. And she said her vision was blurry – like double vision. She started to get very weak and I brought her here."

Sandy nodded. "You say weak, was she falling asleep?"

"No, not that. She just had trouble getting around. And after we were here for a while, and we were talking to the doctor, she started to get even more weak. That thing on her finger – what do you call it?"

"The pulse ox – measuring her oxygen?"

"Yeah, that. It started to drop and the doctor was worried that she wasn't breathing well enough on her own and..."

"I understand."

He let out a heavy sigh. "Have you heard from Barb? Isn't this what happened to her yesterday?"

"Not exactly. I'll let you know as soon as I hear from her. Her symptoms were different."

He sat there, staring into space. "I can't believe this is happening."

"I'm sure the doctor is going to figure out what's going on," Sandy said. "And I'm here to help, too. Other than her being on this diet, did your wife do anything differently recently? Start any new medications, go anywhere?"

He shook his head. "No. Nothing. She lost a little weight, so she was happy about that, but she's just been really busy at home."

"Since she retired?"

He nodded again.

At that moment, a nurse approached them. "Mr. Miller? I want you to know that your wife is stabilized and doing well."

He stood up. "That's good."

"Yes, it is," she said gently. "The doctor wants to speak with you – she'd like to transfer Linda to a hospital in Bellingham. Can you follow me?"

"Of course."

They watched as David walked away and disappeared down the hallway. Jack turned toward Sandy. "So are we going to believe that my food didn't get her sick?"

"I really don't think it did. If that's what she told the doctor, and she was fasting for the whole party, then I don't think that's the cause."

"But what if she drank something?"

Sandy shook her head. "Nope. All of the drinks that you made had a ton of sugar in them. It was very unhealthy, you know."

"Thank you, I do my best."

Sandy stood up and crossed her arms. "I don't think Barb is connected, but we have to talk to her to be sure. It does seem like a strange coincidence that they both fell ill..."

"Has Margie heard from anybody else?"

"Oh! I almost forgot. I'll call her now and give her the update."

Jack stood up. "Do you want me to bring the car around?"

"That would be great," she whispered, pulling her cell phone to her ear.

Jack was happy for any excuse to leave. He didn't like hospitals – to him, it was a place of pain and worry. He'd spent a lot of time with his mother in the last years of her life going in and out their local hospital.

Toward the end, it seemed like she couldn't go even a few weeks without ending up back in a hospital bed.

At the time it was really difficult for Jack, but he was in awe of all the staff that took care of his mom. She became such a frequent flyer that he got to know everybody – the nurses, the medical assistants, even the phlebotomists.

They were so kind and so patient with his mother's failing memory. Not to mention the doctors – his mom had *wonderful* doctors. They always explained things to him so well and treated her with the utmost dignity.

He slipped into the front seat of his car and started the engine. He was happy to get out of that lobby, despite getting to witness Sandy's impressive focus.

The day before, she was dressed as a jolly elf when she effortlessly handled Barb's medical emergency. Jack was so startled that he could barely dial 911, but Sandy didn't seem to need to think twice before hopping into the ambulance.

And today – if there was anyone who could figure out what was going on, it was Sandy. He had full faith in her. It was like watching a composer string together a beautiful symphony – he knew that he was in the presence of a master.

The least he could do was drive the car. He wasn't waiting outside long before Sandy joined him.

"I gave Margie the update. She's horrified, of course – even though I told her that Linda didn't eat anything at the party."

Jack frowned. "I mean, I get it."

"The good news is that she hasn't heard from anybody else. And also, she gave me Barb's address so we can go check on her."

Jack raised an eyebrow. "Oh?"

"And she also gave me Linda's address...in case we need it."

Jack didn't know exactly what that meant, but he wasn't asking questions. He was excited just to be involved.

"Just tell me where, and we'll get moving."

Sandy frowned. "Are you sure? I feel bad making you chauffeur me around."

"Don't feel bad, this is exciting! I mean – it's terrible, but it's exciting to watch you work."

Sandy rubbed her face with her hands. "It would be a lot easier if I could look at Linda's bloodwork or see any of the tests she had done."

Jack shrugged. "I believe in you. Where to?"

They got to Barb's house and Sandy didn't hesitate – she got out immediately, walked toward the front door, and knocked. Jack was a few steps behind her, hoping that he wouldn't have to say anything.

After a moment, Barb opened the front door. "Well if it isn't Mrs. Claus!"

"Hi Barb, it's good to see you again. This is my friend, Jack. Jack, I think you remember Barb from yesterday?"

He extended a handshake. "How could I forget? She made quite an exit from the party."

Barb threw a hand up. "Oh that! I hope I didn't kill the mood."

"Not at all," said Sandy. "I just wanted to check how you're feeling today."

"That's nice of you. I feel fine. Do you want to come in?"

Sandy shook her head. "No – I don't want to be a bother."

She shrugged. "I was told that I should be resting today."

"Can I ask – what did they tell you happened yesterday?"

"They said that I had a mini stroke."

"I'm sorry to hear that," said Sandy. "But I'm glad that you are doing better."

"Yeah, me too. I have to follow-up with a neurologist next week. And you know what? My husband and I realized that this probably wasn't my first mini stroke."

"Oh really?" Sandy asked.

"Yeah! I had an episode like this once before – but it passed so quickly that I didn't think anything of it."

"Good thing Dr. Randall was there," Jack said with a smile.

"Yeah, good thing! I'm glad you're here, actually, because I wanted to apologize for being so...difficult. I don't remember *much* of being in the ambulance, but I think I wasn't very nice."

Sandy laughed. "Please, don't worry about it. That's pretty common after having an event."

"An event like a Christmas cookie party?" asked Jack.

"No," Sandy said shaking her head. "After a neurological event."

Jack shot Barb a smile and she let out a large laugh.

"I think he was pulling your leg, doc."

Sandy turned around to look at him. "I thought you were going to cool it with the jokes for today."

He put his hands up. "I'm sorry! That's it, I'm done."

"Well – thanks for talking to us. The thing is, Linda is in the hospital now. I wanted to make sure there wasn't any connection – it doesn't sound like it's related at all."

"Oh no, is she okay?"

Sandy shifted her weight. "She's not doing great – they're trying to figure out what's going on."

A hand darted to Barb's mouth. "Oh my gosh, I'm so sorry to hear that. I hope that they can figure it out."

"I hope so too." Sandy glanced at her phone. "Excuse us – it looks like I'm getting a phone call."

"Good luck!" yelled Barb.

Sandy answered the phone as she slowly walked back to the car. "Hello, this is Sandy."

Jack watched her carefully. Her expression was unchanged.

"Oh, really? Double vision? Okay...yes. Oh, right – I just spoke to Barb. She's fine, and it's not related, I would say. Okay – right, thanks."

She ended the phone call and stared at Jack. "Bad news. David is starting to have the same problems. The nausea, the double vision."

Jack's stomach dropped. "Now what?"

She leaned back against the car. "How uncomfortable do you feel about being a getaway driver?"

Chapter 11

Jack cocked his head to the side. "I have no idea what you're thinking, but I'm in."

Sandy laughed. Somehow he wasn't sick of driving her around – he seemed totally sincere. But he might change his tune when he heard what she had to say.

"Let's get to the car and talk in private," she said.

"Oh, mysterious."

She smiled but said nothing. She wasn't trying to be mysterious – really, she felt a pang of sadness. She'd enjoyed spending this time with Jack. She was surprised by that – a little shocked, even.

At first she thought that Margie was being way too pushy and obvious about him, and it made her cringe with embarrassment. But Jack didn't seem to mind; he played it all off with that boyish charm.

After having so much fun together, she'd even entertained the idea of seeing him again once they left San Juan. But if she told him what she was thinking now – if he saw the full extent of her craziness when it came to being a doctor – that idea would die.

Her ex-husband got tired of waiting around for her to finish her education. First it was medical school, then residency, then fellowship...he accused her of never prioritizing him. And it was true, to an extent – she had a duty to her patients. But she also believed that she did an okay job of making time for him.

He disagreed. He left her, found someone else, and started a family. It was hard to let him go, but she knew that she wasn't making him happy.

She was just starting her career then. She finally made it through all of her training and had a little spare time. Dating didn't go well, though. She struggled to meet people. She struggled to stay together with anyone for very long.

Her career was exciting and fulfilling, but her love life was always disappointing. That was when she really gave up. It was too hard – it seemed truly impossible to find someone. And she couldn't go through the heartbreak of loving someone as much as she loved her ex-husband and losing them again.

For a moment though, just a *sliver* of time, she had a hope that it might be different with Jack. She thought that maybe they had a tiny possibility to make something new – a second chance.

But it was a fairy tale; she knew that now. It was like going on vacation and wanting to move to the place you were visiting – it was only nice because you weren't working, weren't embroiled in the stresses of life.

He might like *this* version of her – Vacation Sandy. But he wouldn't like the real life version of her, working long hours, and spending so much time on her patients.

Not that Linda and David were her patients...but it was close enough. Now Jack would see the full extent of her madness and go running for the hills.

But it didn't matter. She felt a duty to help them in any way she could.

Once they were settled in their seats, Jack prompted her. "So, what are we doing?"

"Well, just know that you don't have to be a part of this. The issue is that we really don't have much information. I mean – I'm pretty sure that it *wasn't* something at the party because no one else got sick. The fact that two members of the same household are sick suggests that it might be something in their own home, or specific to them."

Jack nodded. "Okay. I think I know where you're going with this."

"Do you?" Sandy bit her lip. "Because it's a pretty crazy idea."

"You want to find them a new place to live, obviously."

Sandy stared at him for a minute. "I know that you're joking, but – "

"I'm sorry," he said closing his eyes. "I swear that was the last one. I'm done."

She continued. "No, what I was going to say is that I need to find a way into their house. You know – to look around. And I just need you to drive me, that's all."

He didn't react at first, but then dug the keys out of his coat pocket and started the car. "Are you assuming that I'll be able to pick a lock?"

"No, I don't think either of us will be able to pick a lock. Actually – I don't know how we're going to do it. It's probably a bad idea. I don't want to break a window or anything."

He shrugged. "I'll break the window. And of course I'm helping, if we go down, we go down together."

"Are you sure that you want to do this?" she asked. "I mean – it's illegal and we may not find anything."

He nodded. "Of course! And wait – couldn't we just ask David if we could look around?"

"Oh," Sandy said. "Is it bad that I didn't even think of that?"

Jack laughed. "I mean – you're kind of a mastermind, but I don't expect you to think of everything."

"No – I just assumed that he would be on his way to the mainland hospital. I didn't want to make him come all the way back to let us into the house. But you're right – we should at least give him a call."

Sandy pulled out her phone and called.

No answer.

She sent a text message and decided to wait for a few minutes.

"So if he doesn't answer in five minutes...?"

She let out a sigh. "Well – if he follows the same course as his wife, he may only have about twelve hours before he's also on a ventilator."

"Yikes! I didn't think of that."

"I know – it's grim. But that makes me feel a lot of pressure to figure this out sooner rather than later."

He nodded. "You're right. How about we just head over? And then...see what happens."

"Okay. See what happens." She shrugged. "That's not a bad idea – maybe they keep a key hidden or something. So the sooner we get there, the better."

"Exactly."

The Miller's house wasn't too far – nothing was really far on this island. And they never ran into traffic like in Boston. It was all quite pleasant – they'd just glide along some beautiful roads for a few minutes until they reached their destination. Sandy didn't think that she'd even seen a single stoplight the entire time she'd been there – was that possible? Did places like that still exist?

They got to the house and parked on the street. There wasn't anyone outside they could talk to – the houses were fairly close together, but it seemed like everyone was locked away. Maybe that was for the better – especially if they started poking around.

Sandy checked her phone again – still no word from David. What if he was progressing even faster than his wife? That would be bad – but at least he was already at the hospital.

Sandy walked up to the front door and knocked. It seemed empty. She peeked into the windows and saw that it was dark. A black cat jumped up onto the windowsill and stared at Sandy from inside.

"Hello – can you let us in?" she asked, holding a finger up to the glass.

The cat watched her with big green eyes. She seemed to be patiently waiting. Sandy was surprised to see that she wasn't scared. Maybe the cat was upset that her people left so early in the morning and in such a fuss. She let out a little meow and Sandy felt her heart melt.

"I think she likes me," she said.

Jack didn't answer, so she turned around to look for him. He was nowhere to be seen. She backed away from the window and went around the side of the house where she spotted him behind a tall bush.

"So I found something interesting," he said.

"Really? What is it?"

He took a step toward the house and reached out an arm, gingerly popping the window open.

"Looks like it wasn't locked."

"Oh." She said. "That *is* interesting."

"Do you think you can get up there? With my help?"

Sandy looked around. There was still no one around. "I think so – quick, give me a boost!"

Jack got down on one knee and motioned for her to use him as a ladder. Sandy got her torso into the window and prepared to lug herself inside when she felt a little push at the bottom of her feet – Jack was still helping.

It was easier to get into the window than she expected and she went toppling inside.

She popped her head out of the window and said, "Stay out there and stand watch."

"No!" he whispered. "Let me in – I can help! I promise!"

She frowned. Sandy didn't want to drag him into this – this was her own scheme.

"Please?" he said.

"All right, fine. I'll let you in the back."

She turned around and saw that the cat had come running into the room. "You're very friendly, aren't you?"

The little cat responded by rubbing herself on Sandy's legs and purring.

"Oh my gosh, you are too adorable. Are you hungry? Come on, help me open the door."

As if she understood, she diligently followed Sandy to a door that led to the backyard. Sandy unlocked it and let Jack step inside.

"Okay, so what are we looking for?"

"Well – anything. Chemicals. Weird seeds – I know that Sandy said she got into gardening now that she's retired. Anything that looks broken – like maybe a broken appliance?"

"Uh – you mean something that could cause carbon monoxide poisoning?"

She frowned. "No – that doesn't make much sense, does it? I mean the symptoms kind of line up – but they wouldn't have both gotten worse after getting to the hospital. They would've died in the house, probably."

"Whoa! That got serious."

"Sorry – you know what I mean."

"I do. Right. I'll start here in the living room."

"Okay. I'll go to the kitchen. Oh – look for medications, too. Prescription drugs or other things. Herbal supplements, diet pills. And look at any kind of alcohol they have in the house – anything homemade or home brewed could cause a problem."

He nodded. "Got it."

Sandy went to the kitchen and decided that she would look methodically from the right side of the room over to the left. She opened every cupboard and drawer.

She found a basket of prescription medications – nothing looked unusual. There weren't even any herbal supplements – sometimes those could be the culprit, but maybe they were somewhere else in the house? She made a mental note to check the bathroom.

She looked at the spices and didn't see anything weird – nothing moldy or with unusual growth.

Under the sink, there were a variety of bottles of cleaning supplies. But again – nothing unusual. Nothing that even was slightly remarkable.

She opened the fridge and studied its contents. There wasn't much in there – Linda was really taking this diet seriously. There were some leftovers from a meal. Sandy picked up the container and lifted the lid – it looked like it was just some old pasta. It smelled fine, nothing bad.

There was a carton of eggs, a container of take-out (past its prime but not suspicious) and in the back of the fridge, there were several glass jars of pickled things.

Sandy gasped. "I think this is it! Why didn't I think of it until now!"

"What is it?" Jack called out.

"Well, actually – it's more common in infants, so I just didn't make the connection."

She grabbed a jar from the fridge and turned to walk into the living room, just as the front door opened and a man walked inside.

Sandy stopped dead in her tracks.

Chapter 12

Immediately, Sandy started talking.

"Oh good, hello! I was just finishing up watering the plants for Linda."

Jack stood frozen in the other room. He could only see Sandy – not whoever just walked in.

"And who are you?" said a man's voice.

"Oh, haven't we met? I'm Sandy, one of Linda's friends."

"I don't know any Sandys." There was a pause. "Looks to me like you're ransacking the place."

Jack cringed – that was his fault. He'd left some drawers open with things that he wanted to show Sandy – just in case she thought something was significant, because he had no idea what he was looking for.

"That was the cat," Sandy said.

Jack knew that he shouldn't make any noise, but it was extremely hard not to laugh at Sandy's comment.

"Oh yeah? If you're Linda's friend, what's the cat's name?"

Oh boy. This guy wasn't bluffable at all. Jack took a step toward Sandy – he couldn't leave her to get out of this on her own.

But almost instantly, she threw a hand up – a subtle signal for him to stop.

"I don't know, I just call her Cat. Listen, Linda asked me to come over here *by myself* and water the plants."

Jack frowned. Was that "by myself" directed at him?

"Gee that's funny, because I'm their neighbor and I'm pretty sure that David asked me to come over here and feed Dolly."

"Right," Sandy said slowly. "Because Linda is in the hospital and they had to leave early to get there. Listen – I'm not a burglar. I'm trying to figure out what made them sick."

"Then why are you holding that, and why did you tell me that you were watering the plants?"

"I didn't want to startle you," she said. "I *do* know Linda, and I am actually a doctor."

"Yeah, and I'm an astronaut," he said with a scoff.

She continued. "I think I know what's making them sick. I need to get back to the hospital."

"Sure lady. You can tell it all to the cops."

"No, please! I think it's these green beans. I think Linda grew them in her garden and then tried to can them and didn't do it right – I think she gave herself botulism poisoning. And David, too."

"Back to the plants, huh? I'm locking you in the bathroom until the cops get here. This is a citizen's arrest!"

Enough was enough; Jack wasn't going to let this unfriendly neighbor get Sandy arrested. He stepped into the room just as the neighbor spun Sandy around and started to push her toward the bathroom.

Jack opened his mouth to yell something but Sandy shot him a look and pointed at the open door. There was enough of a scuffle that Jack was still unnoticed – but he couldn't just leave Sandy there!

"Please," she called out, "the *most* important thing is that the doctor knows that botulism could be causing their illness – every minute counts. We need to call the state – the health department, or the epidemiology office. We need to have the antitoxin flown in as soon as possible."

"Yeah, yeah," he said.

Jack's window of opportunity was closing. It seemed like he needed to get to the hospital right away – but he didn't want to leave her there.

Plus, time seemed slower as he stood, completely panicked. Just before the final push into the bathroom, Sandy flailed a hand wildly at him and yelled, "Go!"

Okay – so she did want him to go. He turned and ran out of the front door and to his car parked on the street.

He didn't go undetected – by the time he reached his car door, he heard a "Hey!" yelled from the house.

Jack looked at him for a moment but didn't stop – he jumped in the car, turned the key and hit the gas.

It took him a while, but there was one message he got loud and clear: this information was time sensitive. Now he just had to get to the hospital and not sound like a crazy person as he explained it.

The drive wasn't long enough for him to calm down – his heart was still thundering away in his chest as though he just escaped a shootout.

But it wasn't all that bad, right? No harm would come to Sandy – well, except for getting arrested. But that didn't seem to bother her much. She even tried to smooth talk the guy as soon as he walked into the house.

Jack chuckled to himself. It was kind of impressive – even though it failed.

He got to the hospital and parked his car – the same spot he'd been in before. Jack walked into the emergency room lobby and saw that it was now empty. It wasn't a very big hospital, and luckily, the same lady was at the desk from when they came in before.

He walked up to the counter, breathless and aware that he was a bit sweaty. "Hi there."

She looked at him and smiled. "Hi! How can I help you?"

"This is going to sound kind of crazy – but do you remember me from before?"

She narrowed her eyes. "I don't think so? Were you here recently?"

"Well I wasn't here as a patient – I wasn't sick. I came here with Sandy – she's a friend of Linda and David Miller."

The woman smiled. "Do you want to take a seat?"

He let a sigh. He'd failed at not sounding like a crazy person. "No, thank you. I'm actually not here to be seen – I need to talk to the doctor about Linda Miller. We think we were able to figure out what is going on with her."

"I'm sorry sir, I can't confirm or deny the identity of any patients, and we can't discuss any patient cases with you."

He frowned. He knew there were a lot of privacy rules – and he had no idea how to get around them. "Can I please see the doctor?"

"Of course. Let me just get some insurance information from you and..."

"No, I don't need to see the doctor for me, I just – "

A woman in a white coat walked into the lobby. "Is everything okay?"

"Oh good!" He said. "Hi, I'm Jack. I was here earlier talking to David Miller."

"Hi Jack."

"Were you the doctor on duty about...three hours ago?"

She smiled. "Yes, why?"

"I know you can't tell *me* anything – but maybe I can tell you something? My friend Sandy and I were here talking to David about Linda getting sick."

The doctor smiled at him. "Do you want to have a seat?"

"No, thank you – I'm sorry, I'm fine. But the thing is – Sandy is also a doctor, and she was determined to figure out what was going on. So we went to Linda's house, and she thinks she found the cause. She said that Linda's been gardening since she retired, and she canned a bunch of green beans, and she thinks that Linda might have given herself botulism poisoning. She said that it was really important that you know right away so that you can order an antivenom? No – sorry, an antitoxin?"

The smile faded from the doctor's face. "Green beans? Is that what you found at her house?"

He nodded. "Yes! And Sandy figured it out – not me. She works with kids, she said it's more common in babies, so she didn't think of it at first. And she couldn't get here but – I needed to tell you as soon as possible."

The doctor stood up. "Well Jack – thanks for stopping in today. I need to make some calls."

"Good luck – I hope it's not too late."

Jack got back to his car and immediately drove back to Linda and David's house. Despite driving a little too quickly, by the time he got to the house, no one was there.

No angry neighbor, no Sandy, and no cops.

Shoot. Now what was he going to do? He didn't have Linda or David's phone numbers – they could clear Sandy of any wrongdoing.

Well, actually, no they couldn't – they were both deathly ill.

He sat in his car for fifteen minutes running through scenarios in his head. He knew that there must be something he could do – maybe Margie could help? He was about to drive to her house when he remembered that she wasn't home.

He pulled out his phone to look up the number for the Sheriff's Department and saw that he had a message from an unknown number.

"Hi Jack – sorry to bother you. This is Margie, Sandy's sister. I haven't gotten any updates from her recently and just wanted to know what's going on."

Bingo!

He called the number and Margie picked up immediately.

"Hello? Jack? Is everything okay?"

"Hi Margie, yes – everything's fine. Well, mostly. I think Sandy figured out what happened to Linda."

"That's great news! What happened?"

"Sandy thinks that Linda gave herself botulism poisoning when she canned some green beans."

Margie gasped. "That's awful! Is she going to be okay?"

"I honestly don't know. But I told the doctor and she seemed to take me seriously, even though I sounded insane."

"Why didn't Sandy just explain it?"

Jack sighed. "That's kind of the problem. We may have done something a little unorthodox...and Sandy might have gotten arrested."

"Jack, is this some sort of a joke?"

"No Margie – for once, I'm not joking."

She laughed. "Well that's a new one. Don't worry – I think I can still call Hank before he gets on his flight to London. I have to go!"

"Okay, thanks Margie."

Jack sat back and put his face in his hands.

Three weeks ago he didn't know where he was going or what he was doing. And now he'd gotten pulled into a medical mystery with a brilliant and beautiful woman, who promptly got herself locked up.

What a trip.

Chapter 13

The bathroom where Sandy was trapped had a small window – too small for her to crawl out of. Not that she was terribly interested in escaping; she thought that she had a much better chance of reasoning with the police when they got there.

At least Jack finally took the hint and got moving. Or maybe he was just running as far away from her as he could because he thought that she was *completely* crazy.

That was a possibility. But no, he wouldn't do that.

Would he?

No. He'd at least stop at the hospital first and pass along the information – he wasn't a monster. But how long would it take him to get there?

And how long would it take for the antitoxin to be flown in? Sandy wasn't sure where it was even kept in Washington state – unlike back home in Massachusetts, where she knew all of the details.

When she was doing her residency, she saw a case of infant botulism. It was terrifying and something that she'd never forgotten. Luckily, the baby fully recovered.

Would Linda and David be so fortunate? If David hadn't progressed into full paralysis yet, then he had a very good chance of a quick reversal...but what about Linda? How many of those green beans had she eaten?

Sandy let out a sigh. Another reason she didn't like diets – vegetables could kill.

She stood up, walked to the door and gently knocked. "Excuse me? My purse is just in the kitchen. May I please have my phone so I can call the hospital?"

No answer.

"Are you still there? If you call David then we could just clear all of this up."

"That's enough! I can't believe that you heard about Linda getting sick and took the opportunity to rob her house."

All right then. He still wasn't happy with her.

There definitely wouldn't be any convincing this man. Sandy gave up and took a seat on the edge of the bathtub. Even if she got her phone, it would be really hard to get the doctor on the line. She could try paging her, but by the time she called back, Sandy might be getting put into a jail cell!

She let out a laugh. She'd never been arrested before – this was quite an extreme situation. Her residents would love it – they always loved a good story.

But truth be told, Sandy didn't care about the arrest or how good the story was. All she cared about was getting David and Linda back to normal. There was a chance that she was wrong and botulism had nothing to do with it. There'd be no harm done – the antitoxin wouldn't do anything.

But if she was right, then the antitoxin would start working pretty quickly. Especially for David. And in her gut, she felt like she'd cracked it.

It wasn't too long before a sheriff's deputy arrived. Sandy could hear them chatting inside the house before they opened the door to the bathroom.

"That's her," the neighbor said, pointing.

"Thanks Hal. I'll take it from here."

Sandy offered a small wave. "Hi there, I'm Sandy Randall. I'm very sorry about all of this, and I can assure you that it's a misunderstanding."

The deputy nodded. "Okay. Come with me and you can tell me your side of the story."

That sounded reasonable – it didn't sound like she was getting arrested yet. She slowly got up from the bathtub and the deputy motioned for her to stop

"Any weapons on you?"

"No sir."

He quickly patted her down, then allowed her to pass. Sandy made her way down the hallway.

"I'm sorry – can I please get my purse? Or – can you get it?"

"Show me where it is."

She nodded and made her way to the kitchen as Dolly pranced in, purring with delight when she saw Sandy.

"It's just there – on the kitchen counter."

"Is it okay if I take a look inside?"

"Please."

He picked up the purse. "Anything sharp that could poke me in here?"

"Oh no – nothing like that."

The deputy used a pen to look around in her purse, at one point pulling out her elf hat and holding it in the air.

"This yours?" he asked.

Sandy had to force herself not to laugh. "Uh, yes sir. That's from my elf costume. I was dressed up yesterday at the Christmas cookie party, where I met Linda. That's where all of this started."

"All right."

She continued. "Linda got severely sick after the party and had to be rushed to the mainland. I talked to her husband, David, at the hospital and came here to look for a possible cause."

"Did you have permission from Linda or David to enter the home?"

Sandy paused. What if she said yes? Would he just let her leave?

But no – she couldn't lie. "Not exactly."

He nodded. "Let's go for a ride."

Oh. Now *that* sounded a little more like she was getting arrested.

Nothing she could do about it now – if the antitoxin worked, she was sure that David would forgive her for sneaking into his house.

If it didn't work...well, she'd have some more time to think about what was causing their symptoms when she was stuck in jail. She followed the officer's directions and took a seat in the back of the police car.

From a purely academic standpoint, Sandy found the entire process fascinating. It was different than what was shown on TV – maybe that was just because she was being cooperative. She really had nothing to hide – and though she knew that theoretically she could request an attorney, she hoped that it wouldn't get that far.

When they got to the county jail, Sandy was placed into a holding cell by herself. It wasn't a very big place, and the only other person there seemed to be a drunkard. He was fast asleep, snoring – though his cell was close enough that Sandy could catch the stench of stale alcohol.

She wondered if she would get a chance to make a phone call – or was that just something that happened in the movies? And even if she did have the opportunity, she couldn't decide who she should call.

She wanted to call the hospital, but she didn't know the number or how to get through to anyone. Her best bet was probably Margie – especially because Margie knew everyone in this town.

Sandy tried to run through other potential diagnoses in her head. Nothing else fit quite as well, but she kept running through ideas. Anything other than having to think of poor Jack.

He had no idea what he'd gotten himself into that morning by agreeing to drive her. At least he didn't also get arrested. Maybe he really did just run off and try to get off of the island as soon as possible – maybe he wanted nothing to do with her again.

That would be fair. She closed her eyes. This was exactly the sort of thing that her ex-husband would get upset about. Linda wasn't even Sandy's patient, yet here she was getting crazed, trying to figure out what was going on.

When it was her actual patients who were sick, and when they were children...there was nothing that Sandy wouldn't do to save them.

A twelve hour surgery? No problem. A forty-eight hour shift? Fine. A weekend spent scouring articles about experimental surgical techniques or medications?

A perfect use of time.

Medicine was her little corner of the world, the sliver where she could actually do something. There were a lot of things that made Sandy despair, but being able to put all of her heart and time into helping one patient set everything right again.

And that was that. Sandy was grateful for the life that she had and what she was able to do with it. And as nice as it was spending time with Jack over the past few weeks, it was a fantasy to think it could continue.

Maybe some people could have it all, but not her. She was happy she could at least have her career. It took her a long time to make peace with it, but she was okay with it now. She couldn't hold it against Jack for having the same realization – hopefully he at least stopped at the hospital on his way out.

After some time, the drunkard awoke and Sandy tried to start a conversation with him. She was bored and wanted to do something to pass the time.

He wasn't interested in talking, though. At first he grunted responses at her, but when she started chatting more, he very loudly told her to "shut it."

Not long after being rejected by him, the deputy who brought her in came back and opened the cell door.

"Dr. Randall?"

She stood up. "Yes?"

"You can come with me. I'm very sorry about this misunderstanding."

"Oh! I'm very sorry as well."

Maybe she was getting out for good behavior?

"I talked to Chief Hank and he let me know everything that I need to know. He also gave me quite an earful for almost arresting his future sister-in-law."

Sandy laughed, accepting her purse from the deputy. "Oh that's right. I didn't even think of name dropping my future brother-in-law."

"He also said that he's never leaving the country again because we're letting the island fall apart in his absence."

"Understandable," Sandy said.

"Do you need help getting home or anything?"

"Ah – no, I think I'll call my niece. But thank you."

"Please send Margie my best!"

"I will. Thanks again!"

Sandy stepped outside and took a deep breath. *Freedom!*

A car honked at her from across the parking lot. She squinted, trying to block her eyes from the sun and see who it was.

The door opened and out came Jack. Her heart jumped. Part of her really did believe that she'd never see him again.

"Hey!" he yelled.

"Hi there." She started walking toward him.

"I can't believe that worked."

"What worked?"

He motioned toward the jail. "I talked to Margie, and she talked to the Chief Deputy Sheriff – who she's apparently dating?"

"Engaged to," Sandy said with a smile.

He laughed. "Oh. Small town, huh?"

"The smallest."

"I'm really sorry about leaving you behind, but – "

"No," she held up a hand. "I'm sorry that I dragged you into this."

"I was happy to help. I got to the hospital as fast as I could, and after doing my best impression of a crazy person, babbling about botulism – "

Sandy interrupted. "Right, as I hoped you would."

He smiled. "Yes, just as planned. And after a while, they decided *not* to admit me for a mental breakdown, and I got to explain everything to the doctor."

"Oh! You got to talk directly to her? That's great."

He nodded. "Yeah. And she thanked me and said she was going to make some calls."

Sandy shifted her weight. "Well – I'm sorry you had to be involved, but thank you for doing that. You might have saved their lives. And I don't want to take up any more of your time, so I'm going to give Jade a call and she can pick me up."

"Oh." He looked at her for a moment. "I really didn't mind – any of it. Even the almost getting arrested part."

"You're too kind, but I know that my..." She paused for a moment, struggling to put her thoughts into words. "My hyper-focus can be a problem. It's just how I am."

"I know. It's great." He pulled his hands out of his pockets and let out a sigh. "To be honest, over the last two weeks with you, I've been having the time of my life."

She laughed. "Yeah, good one."

He took a step closer. "I'm not kidding. I would get arrested with you ten times over if that meant we could spend more time together. You're just...incredible. You're passionate, smart and beautiful and really cool about breaking the law."

She stared up at him and for the first time, words failed her. She thought she could handle anything that life threw at her – but apparently, not this. "I...was not expecting that. I was sure you'd think I was insane."

A strand of hair blew in front of her eyes and he gently brushed it away. "No Sandy – you're a lot of things, but that's not on the list."

Her skin rippled with goosebumps from his touch. "Jack – you're wonderful, really wonderful. But I don't think you understand."

"Oh?" he said, cocking his head to the side.

Why did he do that? It was oddly adorable, like he was an overgrown puppy.

Sandy shook her head, breaking the spell. "This isn't a one-off thing. I mean – it's the first time I've almost gotten arrested, but this is my whole life. Being a doctor – this is what I do. I don't think that – no, I *know* that there's no room for anything else. This is all I have."

She looked at him and watched as her words registered on his face. He frowned for a moment, then his expression softened.

"That can't be true. Because I'm completely taken with you, so now you have that to deal with, too."

She was about to respond when he leaned in, slowly, and kissed her.

Despite her shock at the moment, something stopped her from jumping away – something inside of her told her to enjoy this moment.

When he pulled away, she looked at him. "So...is this your way of telling me that you don't mind giving me a ride?"

He laughed. "Yes. This is my way of telling you that you can have pretty much anything you want from me."

Well. That was *quite* a statement. He continued to surprise her. When she thought he'd run for the hills, he stayed. Instead of ditching her for being intense to the brink of derangement, he joined her. Could it be possible that, after all of these years, she was wrong about him? That she was wrong about her own luck in love, too?

She thought about reaching out to hold his hand but stopped herself. Best to take things slowly. "Let's start with dinner tonight, maybe?"

"You've got it."

Chapter 14

Her famous herb-crusted roast beef would be ready to come out of the oven in twenty minutes and there was still no sign of Sandy. Margie stood in the kitchen with her hands on her hips and debated what to do.

On the one hand, she didn't want to disturb her sister – she was clearly off having the time of her life with Jack. But on the other hand, it was unconscionable for her to miss Christmas dinner, especially since all of the kids were here!

Jade had been over for days, helping with the prep and trying to learn some of the family recipes. Margie's eldest, Tiffany, arrived from Chicago yesterday and Connor, her youngest, arrived that morning.

Her house was filled with good smells, laughter, cookies, and love. And her sister was going to miss it!

"Do you need help with anything else?" asked Jade, popping her head into the kitchen.

Margie smiled and shook her head. "No sweetie – we'll be eating soon if you want to let everyone know."

"What about Aunt Sandy?"

"I was hoping that she'd make it...but I don't want to bother her."

A smile spread across Jade's face. "I can't believe that your plan with Jack worked. Though I don't think Tiffany or Connor will believe any of it until they see him walk through the door."

"Well in that case," she said, reaching for her phone, "we'd better give her a call."

The call went unanswered, so Margie left a brief but cheerful voicemail reminding her sister that her presence was requested for dinner and secret Santa activities.

She busied herself with getting everything to the table, the last of which being the roast beef. Dinner looked quite lovely – she'd even had time to bake some fresh bread rolls, the smell now pulling everyone to the table.

They weren't exactly fresh – she and Jade made them the previous week and froze a batch. Margie was able to pop them into the oven and bake them to perfection. These were the sort of little tricks that Jade really liked and Margie was happy to pass on to her.

Just as Margie was about to sit down for dinner, the front door opened. She dropped what she was doing and rushed to greet her guests.

"Hey sis!" she yelled. "Perfect timing. Merry Christmas!"

"Merry Christmas! I'm *so* sorry that we're late," Sandy said. "We really lost track of the time."

Jack nodded. "Very sorry – I hope that our holiday berry meringue wreath is enough to make up for our rudeness."

Margie accepted the plate from him and pointed above their heads. "Oh no, you're not getting off that easy."

They both looked up to see what Margie was pointing at – mistletoe.

Sandy groaned. "That wasn't there this morning. Did you booby-trap this entire house with mistletoe?"

"Of course! And Connor helped."

Connor yelled, "Sorry Aunt Sandy, she made me!" from the table.

Sandy and Jack looked at each other before Sandy gave Jack a peck on the cheek.

"That was pathetic, but I'll take it," said Margie, allowing them to pass.

All three kids were already sitting at the table and waiting to meet the mysterious Jack.

"Jack, I'd like you to meet my children – Tiffany and Connor. And you already know Jade."

"Nice to meet you all," he said with a smile.

"Hey guys!" Sandy said, going over to hug them all. "Merry Christmas!"

Margie stood at the table and smiled at the scene unfolding in front of her before coming to her senses.

"All right everyone, let's eat before everything gets cold!" she said, passing around the green bean casserole.

Tiffany had about a hundred questions for Sandy – all about the botulism cases, how Sandy figured it out, and of course, Sandy's untimely arrest. Sandy was more than happy to recount it all from the beginning – with Jack's help, of course.

Margie looked on, enjoying hearing the story again. What she enjoyed most was watching Jack as Sandy spoke – he seemed to watch her with such an awe in his eyes. He was truly lovestruck and it made Margie feel absolutely giddy.

Tiffany, however, focused on the botulism. The antitoxin had to be flown to the hospital, which made for a rather dramatic end to the story. Both Linda and David received it, and since David wasn't as far along in his illness, he started to get better almost immediately. Within two days, he was back to normal.

Linda was a different story – the antitoxin worked for her too, but it was much slower. She was finally off of the ventilator and starting to move with the help of her physical therapists. She actually called Margie on Christmas Eve to say that she was thankful that she'd come to the Christmas party. "Thank your sister," she said, "for saving our lives."

Margie promised to relay the message – and reminded Linda that she should give up her new hobby of canning. Linda had no protests about that.

Jack jumped in, giving a rather animated version of how Sandy's confrontation went with the grumpy neighbor. All of the kids were laughing – and now they couldn't accuse their old mom of making up a story about this Christmas match-making gone right.

Margie sat for a moment and enjoyed the feeling of her heart swelling with happiness. The year prior, she was in a much different place – trying to host a disastrous Christmas in her tiny one-bedroom apartment.

And now? It felt like her entire life had turned around. And it seemed like Sandy's life might be undergoing a similar transformation.

Margie took a sip of cider and ripped open a bread roll. Yes, compared to last year, this Christmas was a raging success.

Epilogue

It was the weekend before Halloween and Sandy was on call for another five days; though Friday night had been quiet, she expected things to get progressively more exciting as they got closer to the holiday.

She had one surgery Saturday morning and then made her rounds with the team. She was about to go back to her office and finish up some notes when she received a message on her pager.

She smiled when she saw the number – it was Jack's. Ever since she'd taught him how the pager worked, he liked to ping it every now and again.

She pulled out her cell phone and gave him a call.

"Wow that was fast!" he laughed.

"Well yes," she said. "You do understand the purpose of the pager, right?"

"Yes, very well. This is a stat message. I needed you to know that I'm parked outside of the hospital – if you and your crew would like a free lunch."

"You know that I can't resist tacos. I'll be out soon – and I'll put out the invitation."

"Can't wait to see your beautiful face!"

She shook her head and ended the call. They'd been dating for months and he still liked to sneak things in that he knew would embarrass her. She wasn't *really* embarrassed – no one else heard – but it was enough to make her turn the volume down on her phone.

Not that it mattered. All of her coworkers – from the other surgeons, to the nurse practitioners and nurses, to the pharmacists and the medical assistants and nurses aides – everyone knew Jack and adored him.

After their rendezvous on San Juan Island at Christmas time, Jack decided to move out to Boston and rent an apartment. He reasoned it was only a half hour drive from Helen, that it'd be a better market for his future restaurant and...he wanted to be close to Sandy.

Sandy was a bit surprised by this, but as Margie reasoned, there was no point in trying to stop him. Margie said she should just enjoy it and not worry so much.

And as for the fact that they were crazy about each other and spent almost all of their free time together? Well, that was just a happy byproduct.

When Sandy was at work, Jack explored the local culinary culture and got ideas for what sort of project he wanted to do next. Ultimately, he got the idea to buy a food truck and run a small restaurant out of it. He came up with a number of signature dishes and his popularity boomed.

It was perfect for him at this stage in his life – he set his own hours and could spend the days parked outside of the hospital while Sandy worked longer shifts. He wasn't looking to expand – not yet. He really enjoy the flexibility of being able to spend time with Sandy and Helen.

He insisted that Sandy meet Helen – and his new granddaughter! Sandy felt nervous about it, but it all went exceedingly well. Helen and her husband Phil were enormously kind and welcomed her as if she were part of the family. It was really a brave new world for Sandy and she was glad to have Jack by her side.

After alerting the rest of the team about Jack's generous offer for a free lunch, Sandy took the elevator down and went through the lobby to find Jack's truck parked just across the street.

A line was already forming – he was just too good at what he did. And he spent a lot of time hanging around this hospital, so people quickly came to know and love his creations.

Sandy dutifully waited in line, not wishing to anger any of the paying customers by jumping ahead. When it was finally her turn to order, she stepped up and gently tapped three times on the window.

"Dr. Randall!" He exclaimed, a smile spreading across his face. "What an absolute delight to see you. What can I get for you today?"

"Hm, I think I'm in the mood for a chorizo chicken taco and a side of chips and guacamole."

"Did you catch that Robin?" He yelled over his shoulder. "Can you take care of that while I take a break?"

The young woman nodded. "Of course!"

"Thanks Robin," said Sandy. "How's school going?"

"Oh it's good, really good! Thank you."

Robin was going to college as a premed major – Sandy sat down with her a few weeks prior to talk to her about the options in medicine and some of the various specialties. She was a bright girl – Sandy was confident that she would do well.

Jack hopped out of the truck and gave Sandy a kiss before they walked over to a nearby bench.

"You guys are popular today," said Sandy. "I hope you can handle the influx of hospital employees that are about to come pouring through those front doors."

He laughed. "We're ready. I've got to show my appreciation to the staff."

Sandy looked up, just as a group of seven people walked out of the hospital and over to the truck. "I can confidently say that they feel *very* appreciated every time you stop by."

"And how do you feel when I stop by?"

She smiled. "Happy, I suppose."

"You suppose?"

"Fine – I feel happy."

"Good. And do you also feel full? Of tacos?"

"Yes," she said with a laugh. "I definitely feel full. And a bit, I guess, loved."

"Mission accomplished." He beamed. "You're off Thursday, right?"

"I am. Why, what's up?"

"I thought we could go pumpkin picking. You know, just something really fall-ish. Maybe go for a hayride."

"Do you really want to take a ride on a rickety old tractor? Sitting on a bale of hay – I mean, can we face it?"

He shrugged. "With you I can face anything. But if that sounds too uncomfortable, we can just do the pumpkins."

"I like it when you say that."

"What? That we're going to stick to pumpkins?"

"No." She turned to him. "That we can face anything."

"I think we can. We're a pretty good team, you and I."

Sandy grasped his hand. "We are."

She sat there, taking in the scene in front of them. The sun shined through the golden and red leaves, giving a delicate filter to all of the families and people rushing by on the sidewalk.

It'd been almost a year since she yelled at her patient's mother, causing her to be sent away to think about what she'd done. Luckily, Sandy really *had* just needed a break – and a new perspective, which Margie helped with.

She squeezed Jack's hand and let out a sigh. Life was better than she could have ever imagined – and she was thankful for every moment.

Interested in reading about more love, mystery and adventure on San Juan Island? Check out the rest of the Westcott Bay series – full length novels following Margie, Jade and their friends and family! The first book in the series is *Saltwater Cove*. Included at the end of this novella are the introduction and first chapter to *Saltwater Cove*!

Introduction to the first book in the Westcott Bay series, *Saltwater Cove*

At 48 years-old, Margie Clifton never expected to be starting her life all over again. But when her brother gifts her a property on San Juan Island, that's exactly what she decides to do. After all, it's the perfect place to start a new business venture, provide a second home for her adult children, and recover from her nasty divorce. And if her new life happens to involve the town's gruff and ruggedly handsome Chief Deputy Sheriff? All the better.

The last thing Hank Kowalski wants is an emotional entanglement. It's only been two years since his beloved wife passed, and there's no way his daughter is ready to accept him dating anyone new. Still, there's something about Margie's quiet strength and beauty that draws him in, making him wonder if maybe a fresh start—and possibly a new love—is exactly what he needs in his life.

But Margie is harboring a secret—a dark one that threatens to destroy the new life she's worked so hard to build. Can Margie and Hank find the courage and faith to overcome all that stands between them? Or will their second chance at happily ever after be lost forever?

Chapter 1

The ferry hummed as it slowly made its way towards San Juan Island. Margie zipped her yellow rain jacket before slipping out of the warm galley and onto the ship's deck. The wind tore through her hair and chilled her face, but she didn't mind. She had the deck to herself and a beautiful view of Friday Harbor ahead.

She closed her eyes and took a deep breath. The air was certainly cleaner here than in Seattle. And the sweeping views of the islands were more stunning than what Puget Sound offered, as beautiful as it was. She liked living in the city, of course; it was where she built her life, and where her kids grew up. But her kids moved on and started their own lives, and she finally needed to move on, too.

"Margie? Margie Clifton, is that you?"

Margie took her eyes off of the glistening white sailboats in the distance. "Joan! Fancy seeing you here!"

Joan pulled her in for a hug. "Oh you know me and Ron, always looking for a romantic getaway. How are you? How're the kids?"

"Great, we're all great. And you?"

"Oh, we're all good too."

"Good." Margie paused – she really hadn't expected to see someone she knew, and she didn't want to babble too much.

"Are you just visiting for the weekend?"

And she *definitely* wasn't prepared to answer questions about what she was up to. "No, I uh – actually just bought a place on the island."

"Oh that's lovely! In town, or...?"

"No, on the west side." Ten acres, overlooking the water. But Joan didn't need to know that. It would sound like bragging, and Margie didn't like to brag. She was bursting with excitement, but the whole situation would be hard to explain.

"Oh that's right, your brother lives out here. He flies those little planes between the islands, right?"

"Yeah, that's right! You have a great memory." Technically, he *used* to fly planes between the islands. Now he was – well, that was none of Joan's business. And none of Margie's either, for that matter.

Margie cleared her throat. "Are you and Ron staying in town?"

"Yes, we'll be here for two days, then we're heading up to Orcas Island, and then back home. Just a quick little trip."

"That's lovely." Margie knew that if she kept talking, something would slip out that she shouldn't say, and then she wouldn't be able to stop herself. "Well, it was so nice seeing you, but I think we're getting close to the harbor, so I'd better get back to my car."

"Of course! Lovely seeing you too!"

Margie gave her a quick wave before rushing back inside and down the stairs to her car on the lowest level of the ferry.

She truly did enjoy chatting with Joan – she'd always liked her. Their eldest daughters were only one year apart in school so they always used to run into each other. Joan was a nice person.

"But that doesn't mean you should tell her your life story," Margie whispered to herself as she squeezed into the driver's seat of her Toyota. She promptly buckled her seat belt, then laughed at herself – she wouldn't be able to drive off of the ferry for at least ten more minutes. What did she think buckling her seatbelt would do for her? Keep her safe in case everything turned into bumper cars down there?

She unbuckled herself and cracked the window. Just because Joan was a nice lady and their kids went to school together did *not* mean that Margie should tell her *anything* about the property she bought. That was the one thing that her brother Mike made her promise last month.

"If anyone asks where I am, say I'm working for an airline overseas," he said, handing her a blue ballpoint pen.

"Right, got it." She carefully signed and initialed her name where instructed. Mike explained that he was going back to work for the FBI again, but he couldn't tell her much. She knew not to ask questions. Her brother was nine years her senior, and though she was all of forty-eight years old, he could still make her feel like the baby of the family in situations like these.

"Congratulations," he said when they both finished signing. "You just bought your first home."

She slipped him the $1 bill he'd requested in exchange for the property. "Are you sure I can't pay you something more reasonable?"

He shook his head. "This is all I'll need. Take care of it while I'm gone, okay?"

A voice boomed through the ferry's speaker system. "Drivers, please return to your vehicles and prepare to disembark."

Margie darted a hand into her purse, digging around for her keys. Why hadn't she had the *keys* ready instead of the seatbelt! Finally she found them, trapped under a water bottle. She turned the key in the ignition and waited until it was her turn to drive off of the ferry and onto San Juan Island.

Slowly making her way off of the ship and onto Front Street, she felt a little nervous – she wanted to drop some things off at her new house before coming back into town, but the ferry was a bit late, so she was worried that she might run out of time.

She managed to get through town quickly, though, and made her way to the other side of the island. She wasn't technically taking the "scenic" route, yet it was still gorgeous. There was a quiet peace as she rode past the farms and little houses. Margie rolled her windows down, taking in the cool evening air.

When she reached the beginning of her new property, she had to get out of her car to unlock the chain that blocked the long driveway. She drove up, slowly, as rocks pinged the underside of her car and dust floated into her open windows. It didn't bother her in the least, and soon, she reached the top of the small hill which provided a breathtaking view of Westcott Bay.

It was even more striking than she remembered. The water shimmered delicately against the bright blue sky; puffy white clouds lazily drifted by, visible through the lush green trees on the borders of the property. Margie felt her heart starting to swell.

"There'll be time to stand around and gawk later," she said to herself. She pulled her car up to the house and quickly unloaded a few boxes. She was about to rush back outside when she saw an envelope taped to the back of the front door.

Hey little sis,

I'm really glad you took up my offer to buy this place. It's only halfway a dump, as you can see. I've been fixing it up over the last few months, but it still needs some work. I've left the names of some good contractors I know on the islands. Tell them you know me. Then, when that doesn't work, threaten them as you see fit.

I'm sorry I won't be able to be in touch for a while. I think you'll find that there's something magical about this place. If anything can help you put your family back together...this can.

- Mike

Margie swallowed, trying to break up the lump that formed in her throat. Her brother was not the sentimental type. He didn't share emotions or deal well, for example, with his little sister having a breakdown in front of him.

It was a few months prior that he had to witness it. Margie invited him for Christmas, and everything went horribly wrong. The one toilet in her apartment clogged, she burned the ham, and her downstairs neighbor came up *three* times to complain about how loud they were.

After all the kids turned in for the night, Margie lost it. Mike just stood there, arms crossed, as she cried.

"I'm sorry," she said, gathering empty plates and bits of wrapping paper. "I don't know what's gotten into me."

He stared at her before responding. "It's probably because you're trying to fit your three adult kids and your old brother into a one bedroom apartment for the holiday."

"Well, yes. That's it. That's all. Nothing a little plunger can't fix, right?" She only got to the sink before she started sobbing again. "I don't know, Mike. I don't know how to make it work. I feel like...days like this just make it seem like the divorce has ruined my family. Do you think I can ever make it right again?"

He thought for a moment. "I don't know."

Margie carefully folded the letter and tucked it into her pocket. She couldn't get sentimental right now; she was a woman on a mission.

Inside her purse, carefully zipped into a side pocket, was a photo of a woman. She reached in and pulled it out. There was no way she could put her family back together until she faced this woman from her past.

A woman whose secret was tied to her and her family.

A woman who was, apparently, dead.

Saltwater Cove is available on Amazon now!

About the Author

Amelia Addler writes always clean, always swoon-worthy romance stories and believes that everyone deserves their own happily ever after.

Her soulmate is a man who once spent five weeks driving her to work at 4AM after her car broke down (and he didn't complain, not even once). She is lucky enough to be married to that man and they live in Pittsburgh with their little yellow mutt. Visit her website at AmeliaAddler.com or drop her an email at amelia@AmeliaAddler.com.

Also by Amelia...

The Westcott Bay Series

Saltwater Cove

Saltwater Studios

Saltwater Secrets

Saltwater Crossing

Saltwater Falls

Saltwater Memories

Saltwater Promises

Christmas at Saltwater Cove

The Orcas Island Series

Sunset Cove

The Billionaire Date Series

Nurse's Date with a Billionaire

Doctor's Date with a Billionaire

Veterinarian's Date with a Billionaire

Made in the USA
Columbia, SC
15 June 2023